SAVING THE TELL

A SHAWNEE ADVENTURE

also by

BOB GIEL

A CROW TO PLUCK

SHAWNEE

SAVING THE TELL

A SHAWNEE ADVENTURE

BOB GIEL

HAT CREEK

HAT CREEK
an imprint of
Roan & Weatherford Publishing Associates, LLC
Bentonville, Arkansas
www.roanweatherford.com

Copyright © 2023 by Bob Giel
We are a strong supporter of copyright. Copyright represents creativity, diversity, and free speech, and provides the very foundation from which culture is built. We appreciate you buying the authorized edition of this book and for complying with applicable copyright laws by not reproducing, scanning, or distributing any part of it in any form without permission. Thank you for supporting our writers and allowing us to continue publishing their books.

Library of Congress Cataloging-in-Publication Data
Names: Giel, Bob, author
Title: Saving the Tell/Bob Giel | Shawnee #2
Description: First Edition. | Bentonville: Hat Creek, 2023.
Identifiers: LCCN: 9781633738959 | 978-1-63373-895-9 (trade paperback) |
ISBN: 978-1-63373-896-6 (eBook)
Subjects: FICTION/Westerns | FICTION/Action & Adventure |
FICTION/Thrillers/Historical
LC record available at: https://lccn.loc.gov. 9781633738959

Hat Creek trade paperback edition December, 2023

Cover Design by Casey W. Cowan
Cover art by Frederic Remington (1861-1909)
The Stampede, 1908, Oil on canvas
Interior Design by George "Clay" Mitchell
Editing by George "Clay" Mitchell, Anthony Wood, Lisa Lindsey & Amy Cowan

For Jess

Foreword

WHAT CAN YOU SAY ABOUT Bob Giel that hasn't been said before? I truly enjoyed working with him on the first two Shawnee books and was blessed to be in his presence several times. We were of different generations, but for some reason, we clicked. He was like that great uncle I barely got to know. Bob was a great writer to work with and just a one-of-a-kind person. There were times that we butted heads on how Shawnee's story should unfold, but he told me to be patient and to wait. I never got a chance to tell him that he kept getting better and better as a writer, and that I couldn't wait to see what he had in store for this character in the future. Bob was wonderful, and I wish I had known him longer and had more memories with him. He was taken from us far too soon.

To me, this story is a real classic Western. It reminds me of the days I spent reading other great Western writers like Dusty Richards and Louis L'amour, as well as Marvel's many Western comic books with all the Kids—Kid Colt, Rawhide Kid, Two-Gun Kid. Shawnee would have fit in right along with them.

I'm grateful you're holding this book in your hands today. These tales were important to Bob, and they've become important to so many of us at Roan & Weatherford Publishing—Casey and Amy Cowan, Dennis Doty, Anthony Wood, Chris Enss, and myself. *Sav-*

ing the Tell wouldn't have been possible without them. Bob's family and friends—especially his daughter, Jess, his son-in-law, James, and his granddaughter, Rachel—also provided encouragement, love, and support for his writing, and it shows up in all of his stories. The characters' love and commitment to their families, by blood or bond, is so strong. That had to have come from somewhere. I know he loved each of you, and he felt that love as well.

Happy trails, Bob. Happy trails. You'll be missed, my friend. Until we meet again.

—George "Clay" Mitchell
EVP and Publisher
Roan & Weatherford Publishing Associates

1

THE PLAINS WEST OF THE abandoned Fort Dakota, in the Dakota Territory, were covered with a fresh blanket of snow as Bruno Tell and three local hunters pushed on in search of a buffalo herd known to roam in this area. Bundled in multiple layers of heavy clothing and led by an elderly Lakota guide called Chaska, they moved slowly on horseback. Two pack horses, laden with supplies, brought up the rear, kept in tow by one of the riders. Breaking trail in snow that reached almost to their mounts' knees prevented faster progress. For as far as the eye could see, there was nothing but white save for the leafless, stick-figure trees poking up from the earth below, revealing the dark brown branches and trunks in stark contrast.

The breath emitted from the horses and riders could be seen in the cold. The faces of the men were red from the biting wind and lack of warmth, with splotches of white from the snow, but they pressed on.

The Lakota maintained a distance of a few feet in front of the party. Tell, alone behind the guide, was a horse's length ahead of the three others, who rode side by side.

The center man of the three, a scrawny man with a long, whiskered face looked skyward. "Hey, Tell," he shouted over the howl of the wind. "It'll be dark in a couple hours."

"I know they're out here, Coe," Tell said without turning. His voice was even and gruff. He spoke in a monotone with measured words. "I'm not leaving without them."

Coe grumbled something unintelligible in reply. They continued riding.

Tell was a long, lanky individual, as lean as he was tall. His ruddy, weathered face displayed the result of his years of outdoor life, leathery skin, and multiple age lines. Close to his sixth decade, he still managed to sit straight in the saddle, although it crossed his mind that, in this cold, he might just be frozen stiff.

He watched the Indian carefully for any indication they might be close to their goal. This was his third foray in two years in search of buffalo calves to take back to Texas to run with his herds of longhorns. The eventual union between the two would produce a heartier, meatier animal, increasing its value to cattle buyers and Eastern markets. The idea was not popular with buffalo hunters, who fought tooth and nail to drive off the rescuers. Hence the reason for conducting winter hunts. Summer was the time of the hunter, and any attempt to interfere with their business would be met with anger and bullets.

Dangerous in any weather, finding the herds and separating calves from bulls and cows became even more so during this season since it brought its special set of circumstances. Aside from the problems brought on by cold and snow, winter removed the ability to move quickly to avoid being gored or trampled by the charging beasts.

The necessity of improving his herds to ensure the future for his daughter, Chrissie, drove Tell to these extreme measures. The cattle business was unpredictable to begin with, navigating the fluctuations in the market uncertain at best. Anything that could be done to ensure constancy in the demand for one's product was worth doing. And doing this for Chrissie fell to him. If he didn't do it, no one would. To some extent, Tell believed and practiced conservation. While a noble effort, saving the buffalo would not have been a factor if it did not offer the possibility of enhancing his beeves. And Tell's age entered the equation as well.

Tolls taken by his last two expeditions left him weak and exhausted. This trip seemed even worse. Not that the weather was any harsher. Dakota winters were notorious for their severity, but this one seemed different. Or maybe he was different. Older, less tolerant, maybe even sick? The stomach pains he'd experienced for the last month and a half became more noticeable, more debilitating. He'd tried to ignore it, but it made its presence known more intensely in the last few weeks. He reckoned he'd probably have to deal with it eventually. Just not now.

Now he had too much to do.

If he succeeded in gathering ten calves, he figured he'd have enough combined with the ones already back at the ranch to fully integrate into his herds. Then the rest would be in Nature's hands. But he needed to get this done now, before he lost the ability to hack the rigors involved. He was determined to prevail.

Engrossed in his thoughts, Tell almost did not see the guide raise his hand to indicate a halt. A second later, he pulled back on his horse's reins. Chaska pointed forward to a rise several yards away.

Tell walked his horse to Chaska's side as the Lakota spoke softly, embellishing his words with hand gestures. "Hear buffalo ahead. Wait here."

The three hunters stopped where they were. Chaska walked his horse forward very slowly, ascending the rise and disappearing on the other side.

Tense minutes passed as Tell and the hunters waited in place. Then, slowly, Chaska's head appeared on the horizon as he backtracked to the top of the hill and down to their location. "Little herd," he said quietly as he reached Tell. "Many young."

Tell turned his horse and moved slowly to the hunters. "We do this as we planned. Move in from three sides. Separate the older ones from the calves and drive the herd away. Chaska and I will get the calves."

The hunters split up and started for the rise, separating further as they ascended. Tell rejoined Chaska. They headed straight toward the hill, holding back to allow the hunters time to get into position.

As they crested the grade, they saw the hunters begin their move, riding as hard as the terrain permitted into the buffalo herd, each from a different angle. They shouted, then bared their side arms and fired into the air. The frightened animals bolted and went to a dead run, stampeding away from the noise and activity. As the herd moved, the calves, smaller and slower, separated from the older animals and bunched together in their own desperate bid for escape.

Tell and Chaska urged their horses in pursuit of the young, swiftly circling the dozen or so running creatures. Tell loosed his rope from its tie on his saddle and went into a roping routine of separating individual calves, running them down, and roping them.

While the three hunters kept driving the main herd further away, Chaska continued to circle the calves, heading them into each other to prevent their escape. Tell dismounted and, using short lengths of rope from his coat pocket, tied the fallen calf in place. Then, retrieving his lariat and remounting, he took out after another calf.

This one, a bit older, proved more wily, dodging and careening through the snow toward a gully about an eighth of a mile away. Pushing his horse, Tell swung his loop and tossed it as the calf crested the knoll and started down into the ravine. The rope settled over the calf's head at about half way down the slope. Tell, at the top of the hill, pulled up short, yanking the animal off its hooves.

Intending to hogtie his target in place, Tell dismounted and started down toward the calf while keeping tension on the rope. The calf scrambled up and forward, pulling Tell off his feet. Stubbornly, he held onto the rope and was dragged through the snow onto a level area. The surface under his feet was immediately slippery. A cracking sound warned him too late. Ice!

He clambered to get feet under him. Ahead a few feet, the calf faltered and skidded. The cracking continued. Tell's hand unconsciously held onto the rope as the ice gave way, plunging the calf into freezing water. He hauled back on the rope, pulling the thrashing calf to the side of the opening, where it found purchase on solid ground and scampered up out of the water. He did it! He saved the calf.

The uncertain surface beneath his feet let go in a dull snap. He dropped heavily. The suddenness and the extreme cold sapped his breath as he sank to his chest.

He struggled to keep his head above water, but his saturated clothing weighted him below the waterline. Instinctively, his hands went straight up in a bid for help. Consciousness slipped away, and feeling seeped from his body. The pain in his stomach dulled. His only thought was not to breathe. He had to hold on.

THE VOICES WERE DISTANT. THEY were there, but Tell was not, not completely anyway. And he couldn't make out what the voices said, just that he heard them. He strained to hear and to remember as well.

It all came back to him then. Somehow, he had managed to keep from breathing in that water. Something grabbed him, grabbed his hand and hauled him out. The rest was black. He must have passed out. Shit, that had been incredibly stupid trying to save that calf. Still, if he didn't, who would? And he did it, or at least it seemed so. But at what cost? He might have drowned or frozen to death. His mind wandered, too exhausted to think straight.

"Stoke up that fire."

He heard Coe's voice clearly now. His eyes opened as someone unwrapped the blanket that was around him and tucked another in its place. Likely exchanging dry for wet. There was still a hint of the shivers, but the warmth from the nearby campfire was doing its job.

"Thanks," he forced out in a voice that was almost not there.

"You're back with us," Coe said.

"Sort of." It came out more as a grunt than a statement.

Coe's gloved hand scratched at his stubble. "We was getting worried. You been out for a spell."

Tell looked around for the first time since coming to. The sky was dark and filled with stars. The only light was provided by the flourishing fire close by. It had been about two hours before dark the last he remembered. Now it was completely dark and apparently had been for an untold number of hours. "How long?"

Coe shrugged and looked at the sky. "Must be nigh on to midnight by now, so I don't know—eight, nine hours maybe?"

"Shit. I must be getting old." His thoughts drifted to Chrissie. He'd set out to do this for her, for her future. And here he not only damn near got himself killed, he failed in his duty to her. Last he knew, there were only two calves. "What about the calves?"

"Yeah, we got 'em for you, ten of 'em. Got 'em hobbled yonder."

Tell breathed a sigh. He'd chosen well when he hired Coe. He could trust him. The other two were just in it for the pay, having been engaged by Coe, but there was more to Coe than working for a wage. "Thanks. You boys're a godsend."

Coe grinned. "Well, I ain't so sure 'bout that, but if'n you say so. You about ready to call this done?"

"It's done."

"Good. We'll head for Fort Dakota come morning, if'n you're able."

Tell looked away, steeling himself. "Yeah, I'll be able."

THEY KEPT TELL WARM AND fed him broths concocted by Chaska. He slept through the night and awoke well after sunrise to the noise of the camp being broken down. Through sleepy eyes, he watched as the pack horses were loaded. Coe looked around as Tell tried to raise himself on an elbow and found it difficult because of the blanket wrapped tightly around him.

"Coe." His call was feeble.

Coe turned from his work. "Morning, Tell. You hungry?"

Tell shook his head. "Yeah, starving."

Coe went to the edge of the fire and picked up a frying pan that contained sizzling bacon strips and brought it over to Tell. A wan smile crossed Tell's lips. He accepted the pan and set it on the piled blanket on his lap. The food was gone in a few short minutes.

"Think you can sit a horse?" Coe asked. "Or should we rig you up a *travois?*"

Tell threw off the blanket and forced himself to unsteady legs. "If I can't sit a horse, tie me on. I'm not getting drug anywhere."

"Suit yourself," Coe said.

Swaddled in the clothes that had dried on his body overnight and an additional blanket, Tell was helped into the saddle. He hung on tightly to the saddlehorn. Complete with the ten buffalo calves, they set out for Fort Dakota.

The full day trip put them at the fort at dusk. Activity there was almost nonexistent as they rode into the eighteen building complex erected on the bank of the Sioux River at the location of the Sioux Falls. Having been vacated by the military a year earlier in 1869, the fort, more on the style of a village than an armed forces installation, was now occupied by a few hunters and settlers.

With Coe leading and Tell clinging to the saddle, they made their way to the enlisted men's barracks. Two of the hunters took the horses in tow and saw the calves secured in a makeshift corral nearby. Coe and the Lakota helped Tell inside into a bunk and piled blankets on him while Chaska stoked up the fire. A few occupants at the far end of the building paid no heed to this new activity.

Food was brought to Tell. He ate voraciously and, shortly after, experienced stomach pains, which he passed off to himself and others as indigestion from consuming too much too fast. He slept well into the next day.

Coe entered the building as Tell rose from the bunk.

"Feeling better?"

Tell sat heavily back on the bed and pulled on his boots. "Some. Food and sleep made a difference."

"I ain't no sawbones, but I'd say you need to rest a few days 'fore you heads for home."

Tell nodded. "I'm not in any shape to disagree. Not sure I said this before, but thanks for pulling me out of that."

"You done said it. You'd a did the same, no doubt."

"Still, I owe you more than our agreement."

"That's up to you, Tell. I ain't refusing, but I don't charge for a man's life."

Tell pulled a leather poke from his shirt pocket. "I know, but it's right to do." He pulled the leather drawstring open and dug out gold coins. Counting out the amount he'd ciphered, he dropped the spares back in and handed the money to Coe. "There's a hundred and a half there."

"Thanks a heap, Tell. More'n enough to take care of the others and then some." Coe pocketed the coins and started for the door. "I'll be around, you need me."

As Coe stepped out, Tell attempted to stand. Another sharp pain in the stomach area put him back down in a sitting position. He gasped and bit his lower lip to distract himself from the pain until, moments later, it subsided. "Damn it!" Still, he could not give in to it. He had to get those calves home to Texas. The project had to be seen through. For Chrissie. It had to.

Tell spent three days resting, during which time his stomach bothered him intermittently. On the fourth day, he prepared to set out for Texas, hitching the two pack horses to his Conestoga wagon and securing the ten calves and his saddle horse to the rear. He had come using this conveyance, and this was how he would make it home.

Outside a makeshift stable near the barracks building, Tell finished his work on the wagon.

Coe approached. "Need some help?"

"'Bout done." He made the last connection on the whiffletree.

"Don't mean to pry or nothing, but I'm powerful curious. What're you fixing to do with them calves?"

"Past two years, I've been running them in with my beeves. They make a heartier, meatier steer. Cattlemen's Association put me onto it. Said some ranchers out west and up north started doing it after the war. Seems to work."

Coe pushed his floppy hat back and scratched at his head. "Well, I'll be... I'd a never guessed that."

"Surprised the hell out of me as well, but I'll try anything to build up my spread. I'm the only kin my daughter's got. Want to make it better for her."

"Reckon if I had a kid, I'd be doing for her like you're doing. I wish you luck with it."

"Thanks. You expect you'll be here next year? I might need to come back."

Coe pulled his hat back down and shrugged. "Could be. A few of the settlers hereabouts is making talk about setting up a town near the falls. If that happens, I'll head west and follow the buffalo. I ain't much for towns and the like."

"Well, if I do come back, I'll look for you. And if you're ever in Texas, come by the Tell Ranch outside of Fort Worth. You'll be welcome, always."

They shook hands. "You never know. I might just do that."

Tell climbed aboard the wagon and put the team in motion. Coe stood and watched as it disappeared into the snow-covered horizon, heading south.

2

A WEEK AND A HALF into what Tell estimated to be a three-week trip took a toll on the man. The monotony of driving the team and the discomfort of his stomach distress were interrupted only by the frequent glances he made behind him, through the rear opening in the wagon cover, to ensure the calves were still there. He'd done this the only way he saw would work. He'd tied the calves in a line attached to the back of the wagon, two abreast, five in each queue. Several times along the way, they'd gotten tangled up. The drag on the wagon, as they struggled, made him stop and get them back in their lines. Each time, he checked the integrity of the rope. It held until, somewhere in Indian Territory, a break occurred. Five calves, strung together at the necks, wandered off away from the wagon. Tell's glance over his shoulder was his first indication and all he needed to haul the team to a stop. Shit!

He wrapped the reins around the break handle and dropped to the ground, wincing at the pain in his stomach. In a second, he was in the saddle, taking off after his quarry. The freedom the fleeing calves experienced put speed in the hooves. The only thing keeping them together was the rope. That would soon succumb to the constant tugging. Tell rode hard to run them down, making the gut pain worse.

As he reached them, they veered and collided with each other, presenting an obstacle in front of Tell's cow pony. The suddenness caused the horse to shy, to rear. Unprepared, Tell lost purchase with the saddle and landed hard on his back on the cushion of a bush. Not much of a buffer but enough to prevent injury. He watched, somewhat helplessly, as the calves wandered on their own path. Rolling to his knees, the sound of the calves' hooves faded, to be replaced by the approach of another, one set of steady, galloping beats. Tell glanced toward them to see a big, dark gray horse carrying a rider in ranch clothes and a wool coat heading for the calves. In the back of his mind he recognized that horse and maybe the rider as well.

The intruder came on, riding in circles around the young buffalo until, exhausted, confused, they bunched together and settled down. Stopping the horse, the man dismounted and seemed to whisper something to the gray. He walked away from the horse toward where Tell knelt. The gray worked to keep the calves together as the man reached Tell.

Tell's eye widened as recognition took hold. He knew the horse, or thought he did, but one look at the man's face made him certain. "Shawnee?" There was disbelief in his voice.

The young man stopped dead, studying the downed man. It took a second. "Mister Tell?" His incredulity equaled Tell's.

They stared at each other for the better part of a full breath. Shawnee's hand extended to pull Tell to unsteady feet. Their blurts occurred at the same time and so were unintelligible. Laughter and glad-handing followed as the two expressed surprise.

Calming, Tell spoke the first understandable words. "I never thought to see you again."

Shawnee nodded. "Mighty well told."

"What are you doing out here in the middle a nowhere?"

Shawnee shrugged. "Oh, you know, just passing through."

Tell shook his hand again. "Well, you surely showed up in the nick a time."

"I reckon. Say, what's going on? What're you doing out here in the middle a nowhere?"

"Trying to get these calves to the Tell. Been on the trail a week and half, and they appear to be getting the better a me."

Shawnee looked over at the calves, still being wrangled by Gray. His hand went to the back of his neck. "Them's buffalo!"

"That's right. Buffalo to run in with my beeves. Give me a hand to get 'em tied to the wagon, and I'll tell you about it."

"Sure thing."

Tell retrieved his horse and, together with Shawnee on Gray, wrangled the wayward calves back to the wagon. Tell filled in his young companion on the theory of integrating buffalo with cattle to improve the herds.

Shawnee secured the knots tying the calves in line. "Well, don't that beat all. And you're trying to get 'em back to the Tell all by your lonesome?"

Tell secured his horse to the wagon. "I am."

Shawnee flashed a smile. "Well, sir, I'd be proud to side you if you'll have me."

Tell grinned. "I will, and welcome."

Shawnee mounted Gray as Tell climbed aboard the wagon. The journey continued.

BUNDLED IN A SCARF AND a wool coat, Cletus Workman led his crew over the south range of the Tell Ranch, rousting stray cattle out of the brush as they went. Beeves was sure a dumb lot, wandering away from the protection of the herd, getting lost in the bushes and such. Think they'd learn better, but no, they still needed finding as much as they needed tending.

His black skin glistened with sweat. He had always perspired more than most, and a working cowboy just seemed more prone to it because his labor was physical. It didn't matter much that it was winter or that even Texas got pretty cold in that season. A cowboy still worked up a sweat, no matter when or where.

Tall and broad, Cletus had a round face and the blackest of skin. He sat a horse as if he'd been born to it. He'd been foreman of the Tell for must be nigh onto ten years now, ever since Mr. Tell bought him from that slave trader in New Orleans and gave him his freedom. They formed a bond early on. Grateful for the chance to be free, Cletus worked hard to overcome his shortcomings. He couldn't read or write, but he fixed that. And proved his worth as a leader. Mr. Tell must have saw something in him when he made him foreman, and by God, Cletus's determination made it work.

As the half dozen men, spread out over a three hundred yard stretch, reached the edge of the south range, Cletus made a last scan of the area. "That's it. We done," he called in a deep, resonant voice. "Head on back." A wave of his hand got the message to those riders who were not within hearing range. They turned and started back the way they had come, joining together as they progressed. Within a half mile, they reached the twenty-odd strays that had been bunched together and held in place by two of the hands. Cletus made a forward sweep with his hand. "Head 'em back to the herd."

The crew turned the steers and urged them north. They moved for half an hour and reached a meadow where the main herd grazed contentedly. After integrating the strays into the herd, Cletus assigned the nighthawks, whose job it was to keep the cattle in check overnight. He led the remaining members overland toward the ranch headquarters.

It was late afternoon as they rode in. Cletus glanced to the northwest. Movement had caught his eye a second earlier. Coming down the hill, the wagon carrying Tell lumbered along, leading the buffalo calves. Cletus got the impression from Tell's posture on the seat that the man was more than weary, a lot more. With a smile on his face, Cletus left the cowboys and headed off to meet his boss and benefactor. He reached a gallop by the time the wagon descended the grade to level ground.

A single rider appeared from behind the wagon and rode up alongside Tell. The rider and the horse were familiar instantly, but, naw, that couldn't be. Or could it? Cletus pulled rein to get a steadier look. And it was—Shawnee and Gray. Cletus continued toward the wagon, waving his hand. "Mister Tell!"

Tell looked up and made a weary acknowledging gesture. Cletus pulled up sharply at the wagon and took a closer look at the man. His observation was that Tell was beat to shit.

"How do, Cletus." Shawnee's greeting took Cletus's attention.

"Shawnee? What the hell you doing here?" He rode to face Shawnee and gripped an extended hand. "I didn't never think to see you again."

Shawnee grinned. "Reckon you never know. How the hell are you, anyhow?"

"Fine and dandy." Cletus turned his attention back to Tell. "More'n I can say for you, boss. You looks plumb tuckered."

"Long trip," Tell said. "Glad it's over." He kept the wagon moving, heading for the main house, as Cletus and Shawnee rode alongside. The rest of the ride was done in silence. Tell stopped the wagon outside the house and wrapped the reins around the brake handle, pulling a half-hitch in place. Exhausted, he climbed down. With his back to Cletus and Shawnee, who had pulled up nearby, he faltered and reached out to support himself on the wagon wheel.

"Mister Tell." Cletus dismounted. "You all right?"

Tell took a deep breath and steadied himself. "I'm... just dog tired is all."

Cletus put a hand on his shoulder. "You go ahead on inside. Me and the boys'll take care of things out here."

Tell nodded. He leaned away from the wheel and moved on uncertain legs around the team and into the house. Cletus watched him until he was inside, hoping Tell was indeed just dog tired.

Shawnee dismounted and came closer to Cletus. "He don't look like he's just tired."

Cletus nodded. "Yeah, they's more to it, but knowing Mister Tell, he won't say nothing, and we better don't ask."

"Well, I didn't plan to come back here, but when I seen how poorly he looked, I ciphered I should ought a. Not looking to run into Chrissie neither, but long as I'm here, anything I can do to help?"

Cletus looked over his shoulder. "Just so's you know, Chrissie ain't here. She away at school. Them buffalos need to get put with the beeves. You reckon you can take care a that?"

Shawnee nodded. "I'll do 'er. South range?"

"Shit, it's like you never left."

Shawnee mounted. "Yeah, well...." He directed Gray to the rear of the wagon, loosed the calves' ropes, and led them away.

Cletus hailed the cowboys near the bunkhouse. "Hey, some of you boys come on and help me here."

As the hands started toward him, Cletus stared at the house, preoccupied with concern for Tell's health.

Morning brought further worry as Cletus assembled his crew for the workday. It was cold again, more noticeable because of the slow rising sun. The cowboys were bundled for warmth. They entered the corral to saddle up.

Tell appeared on the porch of the house, dressed ready to ride.

He started toward them. "Cletus, I'm coming with you." His voice was still somewhat weak but possessed its usual commanding presence. He walked slower than usual.

Cletus left the corral to meet Tell halfway. "Ain't no need you going, Mister Tell. You needs to rest up. Me and the boys can handle things."

"I'm still the Tell in the Tell Ranch." Tell kept walking. "I spent the better part a two months away. I'll be looking in on things. Have someone saddle my horse."

"Yes, sir." Cletus spoke to the spot where Tell would have been had he stopped. He turned and followed Tell. "Terry," he called to one of the hands. "Go ahead on and saddle up Old Ringo."

Terry hurried toward the barn as the other hands finished saddling and mounted up. Shortly, Terry brought Tell's horse to him. Tell took the lead, heading west.

They spent most of the morning locating and rounding up strays. As they rode, Cletus watched Tell. Watched him slump a little further forward in the saddle as time passed. Watched him double over in pain and grip his stomach, then shoo away any help the hands offered. He grunted. "I'm all right. Get back to work."

Cletus let it go, not wanting to expand the incident, but it added to his concern and his questions. What was ailing Tell? Why was he not seeing to it? Cletus shook his head, confused by Tell's actions and his seeming lack of interest in his health. It was obvious this last trip took more than its toll on the boss. At some point, as dangerous as that ground might be, Cletus knew he would have to speak up.

Not here. Not now. But soon.

―――――――

FOR THE NEXT WEEK, CLETUS observed Tell without being obvious about it. He saw the weakness, the pain Tell experienced, but he held back. Past incidents told him Tell was his own man. He made his own decisions and tolerated no interference. This needed to be handled delicate-like, something Cletus was not sure he had the wherewithal to pull off. He continued to watch.

A few days later, Tell spent the day alone on the range surveying ranch operations. Cletus followed his boss, keeping far enough away to stay out of Tell's sight. He counted on the fact that Tell would not expect to be tailed and would be concerned enough with his task to pay no heed to anything else. It worked.

A couple hours into the mission, Tell pulled up in an open area, doubled over in the saddle. Cletus crested a knoll and stopped short at the sight. He wrestled with the question of whether or not to move in and help. Tell fell across his horse's neck. His feet out of the stirrups, he slowly slid out of the saddle and dropped to the ground on his back.

That was it. Cletus waited no longer. He raked his spurs across his horse's flanks and went to a gallop down the slight grade, coming to a sharp halt near where Tell lay. A hurried dismount, accomplished before the animal stopped, put him at Tell's side. He dropped to a knee as Tell turned his head at the disturbance.

"What—" Tell did not finish his question.

"Lay still, boss. You ain't well. I going to get you home."

"What the hell are you doing out here?" Tell had to grunt the words out.

"I done followed you. You ain't been well since 'fore Dakota. Time you seen to it."

"It's nothing. I'm just tired is all."

"You more'n tired, Mister Tell. That for sure and certain."

"I got some misery in my belly, I'll give you that. Bad food, I'd say."

"You got to see to it, whatever it be. Ain't getting no better."

"Cletus, I'm telling you, I'm all right. Now back off."

Cletus sucked it up and dove in. "I can't do that. You done been a friend to me when nobody else would. Done pulled me out of that slaver's hands, trusted me, treated me better'n any man should a. Time for me to do you back. I'm taking you home, and I'm sending for the doc. I ain't going to let you being stubborn make you sicker. Now, you can fire me, you got a mind, but I ain't backing off."

"Cletus—"

"No more, Mister Tell, no more. Don't you fight me on this. I stronger'n you. Now, I picking you up and getting you home."

Tell nodded submission. Cletus helped him up and back into the saddle. "Lay yourself cross his neck and hang onto his mane." Tell complied. Cletus remounted, picked up Tell's horse's reins, and led the way back to the ranch house at a slow pace.

Later that day, Cletus paced the ranch house porch impatiently. After getting Tell to bed, he'd sent Terry into Fort Worth to bring the doctor back. He now waited for their arrival.

As he reached the center of the porch for the umpteenth time, movement in the distance caught his eye. He looked out at the trail leading in from the main road to see two riders approaching. At this point, they were too far off to identify, but the ranch didn't get many visitors, so he made the assumption that the two were Terry and the doctor. He stood there waiting as they advanced.

Moments later, the two riders were close enough for Cletus to make them out. One was indeed Terry. There was no mistaking his wide frame and worn range clothes.

The other man was tall, that was evident even though he was on a horse. Terry had a fair amount of height, but this man was a good head above him. He was thin and wiry with a long face that was partially covered by a well-trimmed growth of beard around his jaw line. The face was light in coloring. His hair was a dark blond, slicked back neatly. His suit of clothes and overcoat were dark, as was his homburg hat. He carried a black satchel.

As they drew near, Cletus noticed the simple saddle on the tall man's horse—nothing more than a slab of leather with no adornments at all, something akin to the types he'd seen used by the military.

To Cletus, this could be no one other than Dr. Ramsey. He had seen the man from afar a few times in Fort Worth, never to talk to. Cletus had been impressed with the way he carried himself.

The two men pulled rein at the hitch rail in front of the house.

"Cletus," Terry drawled. "This here's Doctor Ramsey." He spoke as the doctor dismounted.

Cletus moved to the edge of the porch. "How do. I be Cletus Workman, Mister Tell foreman."

"How do you do." Ramsey had a distinctly British accent. "I understand Mister Tell is ailing."

Cletus recognized the man's manner of speech, having heard it several other times in his life. "Yes, sir. He got a misery in his gut. He ain't doing good at all."

Ramsey smiled a little. "Well, then, let's have a look at him, shall we?" He wrapped his horse's reins around the rail.

"He inside." Cletus went to the door, preparing to open it as the doctor stepped up onto the porch. "He done told me he fell into freezing water a couple weeks back."

The doctor acknowledged the fact with a long, "Hmmm!"

As they entered, Ramsey removed his hat. Cletus led the way up the staircase to the second floor. Tell's bedroom door was in front of them as they reached the landing.

Ramsey went to the door. "Please wait here."

Cletus moved closer to him. "I should ought to be in there. I been his foreman better'n ten year now, most close to a son as he got. Mister Tell daughter away at school. She being the onlyest kin he got and she being not here, and he ain't been right of late, and he ain't taking kindly to me calling you in, so's I should ought to be in there."

The doctor gave that some thought. "Oh, very well, but if he overrules it, you will have to leave."

"Yes, sir."

Tell offered no objection to Cletus remaining during the examination. The only protest he made was that he had to withstand the doctor's poking and probing as well as the questions the man asked. How long were the stomach pains present? Where exactly were they located? How long was he in that freezing water? He answered the queries as best he could, and he grunted and winced when Ramsey manipulated his belly. The pains were in his lower gut and had been present for about a month, but truth be told, he could recall twinges starting several months before that and increasing steadily. They came and went at random. He was pulled out of that hole in the ice within seconds, or that was his recollection anyway. They made sure he was warm and dry, but even at that, he'd had the shivers ever since. Getting and staying warm had become a chore, which had never been an issue before.

Cletus stayed out of the way, but he kept his eyes and ears open, watching the doctor lean over the bed to work on Tell. He knew it was difficult for Tell to be forthcoming about anything in his personal life. Silently sucking it up and going on, that was his way. Cletus was surprised Tell told the doctor as much as he had. Likely he was kowtowed by the doc's imposing way.

"Well, Doc, what's your verdict? What's ailing me?"

Ramsey hesitated. "I would prefer to do some further research before rendering a diagnosis. I have some ideas, however, they are just that, ideas. These pains you experience do not seem a common occurrence. I fear they are not simply what one would term a belly ache, but I hesitate to conclude anything until I'm certain."

"So, what you're saying is, you're as much in the dark as I am. And you're the doctor."

"I apologize, Mister Tell. I don't wish to alarm you unnecessarily. Please allow me a few days to look into this."

"Why, sure, Doc, take all the time you need." Tell's statement sounded sarcastic.

Cletus reckoned it likely was.

Ramsey pulled a small bottle with a cork stopper from his bag. "This is laudanum, for the pain. Follow the directions written on the vial." Ramsey placed the medication on the night table and closed his bag. He reached to the bed for his hat and coat. "I'll return as soon as possible."

"Right." Tell turned away as he spoke.

Cletus took that to be more sarcasm.

The doctor pulled on his coat and went to the door. As he passed Cletus, he reached his hand to Cletus's arm and made a gesture with his head for Cletus to follow him. They stepped out, and Ramsey closed the door. Going down the staircase together, the doctor spoke quietly to Cletus. "You must realize that Mister Tell is very ill."

"How much ill you talking?"

"As I mentioned, I must research this before I can be certain, but the stomach pains concern me to no end. This is definitely more than a simple ache. I felt something there, something that should not be there. You spoke of Mister Tell's daughter earlier."

"Yeah?" Cletus said as they reached the first floor.

"Are they close?"

Cletus was puzzled by the question, but he answered all the same. "Like I said, he ain't got no other kin but her. They close."

"It might be advisable to summon her home to be with her father."

"You reckon it be that serious?"

"Yes, Cletus, I do. I'll know more in a few days, but... yes, I do."

Cletus was stopped cold. He felt a chill dart up his spine at the thought of Tell being that bad sick. He thought to ask more of the doctor, but he held back, not really wanting the answers. "I'll send for her right off."

Ramsey placed his hat on his head. "Good man." He went to the front door.

On the porch, Cletus watched him mount and ride away. He glanced back at the house, in deep concern for his boss, then stepped off to head for the bunkhouse to fetch paper and a pencil, shaking his head as he walked. He had to write out the telegram he would send to Chrissie. This was one of those times when he was glad he'd learned to read and write, but still, he'd have to ponder hard on what he would say.

3

IT WAS MORNING. CHRISSIE TELL prepared for her classes. She made last-minute adjustments to her clothing and picked up the black leather briefcase from the bed. A slight framed girl, she carried herself straight. Her light red hair was piled in curls off her neck. A simple brimmed hat was pinned in place to her hair. Freckles covered her round, delicately featured face. She wore a dark, knee-length wool coat to shield her from the winter cold she would enter for her short journey to the main building and her first class.

In black, highly polished, calf-high boots, she left her room on the third floor of the housing facility at Charnwood Institute in Tyler, Texas, heading for the start of her day. She had been quartered on campus since September 1869. Her status as a freshman now neared its end. It had been six months since her arrival, and in that time, she'd excelled at her studies and was on track to be listed in the school's prestigious honor society.

As she walked toward the staircase, her mind drifted back to the Tell, her home. She missed home and her father. It had been a difficult transition when she arrived at Charnwood, an outdoor girl accustomed to simple dresses or range clothes. Here, she had to conform to a strict dress code and proper decorum. It took some adjusting, but she managed to fit in. Initially rebellious at the change, she finally realized Pa was right. She was growing up in a changing world, and he wanted her ready to meet it. Buckling down, she did the work. The results were evident. Still, she looked forward to the end of the school year and the ability to go home and unwind.

She descended the stairs to the first floor lobby in an elegant manner, the briefcase tucked under her arm.

"Miss Tell." The voice behind her was that of Miss Ward, the middle-aged spinster who managed the building. "Christina, wait."

Chrissie turned to see a tall, gaunt woman in a gray dress approaching her.

Miss Ward held a slip of paper in her bony fingers. She extended her hand to offer the paper to Chrissie. "This telegram just arrived for you."

"Oh, thank you." Chrissie's voice was soft and expressive. But a telegram? Who was it from? Pa? She'd received a letter or two from him, but they were just hellos and expressions of love. Telegrams were important, even urgent.

She took the yellow page and opened it. As she read it, the look on her face changed from the perpetual smile she usually exhibited to one of deep concern.

Miss Crisee

Your father is bad sick. He will not rest like he should. Please come home. Talk some sense in to him like only you able.

Cletus

Chrissie stood there staring at the page. She recalled the stubbornness Cletus alluded to, the time many years earlier when Pa tried breaking a particularly wild horse. It took him all day and an injured back, but he prevailed. That same tenacity that helped him build the Tell might now be his undoing. Chrissie's sky blue eyes noticeably filled with tears.

"What is it, my dear?" Miss Ward placed a comforting hand on her arm.

"It's my father." Chrissie's voice was shaky, and a tear streamed down her cheek. "He's ill. I've got to go home immediately."

"Of course. You go up and pack. I'll see to everything here."

"Thank you, Miss Ward." Chrissie went back to the staircase and started up. Miss Ward would make her excuses to the school and see that whatever work was missed by her absence would be collected and held for her. There was no question about this because, on several occasions in the past, Miss Ward had gone out of her way to care for the girls in her charge. Chrissie expected no less in this case.

As she climbed the steps, Chrissie tried to get her emotions in check. She had to meet this challenge head-on, the way Pa would, the way he'd taught her. This was a test. If it hadn't happened, life would have gone on uninterrupted. Classes, lectures, and exams would have continued. But it *did* dome up, and it had to be dealt with in an intelligent, organized manner. This she resolved.

She needed to pack only what she absolutely needed for the trip to Fort Worth. A list of those things formed in her head by the time she reached the first landing. She burst into the room with a flourish, tossed the briefcase on the bed, and fetched her carpet bag from under the bed. Quickly, she shoved the few things she'd take into the case. No time to change. She had to get to the stagecoach station as soon as possible. Oh, God, please let him be all right.

THE TWO-DAY STAGECOACH JOURNEY from Tyler to Fort
Worth was uncomfortable at best, covering rough country that tested the rudimentary suspension of the coach. As Chrissie endured the
endless bumps and ruts, her thoughts drifted back to a happier time.
She was a little girl, maybe five or six, seated on a saddle on a particularly gentle horse. Her father sat behind her with his arms around her
waist, while in front of her he held the reins in his hands. The bounc-
ing of the coach reminded her of the rhythmic jostling of the horse
as it moved along a dirt trail. A stern but kind man, her father gave
her whispered advice to make the ride more pleasant. "Don't fight the
horse. Go with his movements."

Then reality brought her back to the reason for her trip. What
was this illness? How serious was it? Did it threaten her father's life?
She resolved to get the answers to these questions as soon as she
reached home.

Spending the halfway point at a way station in the middle of
nowhere, the passengers found that it boasted few amenities other than the security of being indoors at night. The stop provided
the coach with a fresh team and the travelers with a hot dinner of
sloppy, tasteless stew and very little else. There were no rooms or
even any beds available. If they slept at all, they curled up in wooden
chairs or on the floor in front of the fireplace.

Chrissie was one of those who chose a chair. Her twenty-year-
old body was capable of contorting into something akin to a ball.
She found a fairly acceptable position and waited patiently for sleep
that never really came. Dozing and waking for most of the night was
as good as it got.

In the morning, the other three passengers rose at about the same time as Chrissie did. With the bright rising sun shining through the cabin windows, no one found it possible to pursue slumber further. Groans, yawns, and some cursing followed as they came back to life. Sounds of cooking in the kitchen next door clinched it. The racket negated any thoughts of sleep that still existed.

As she extricated herself from the chair, experiencing aches and pains from the lengthy, awkward position it forced, Chrissie thought back to the previous September when her father brought her to Charnwood. They traveled in his smoother-riding buggy and stayed the night in a hotel in a town midway between the ranch and the school. It was infinitely more comfortable than this travesty.

This, however, was what she had to endure to get back to the ranch alone. Resigned to it, she freshened up as best she could and consumed the provided breakfast, fried eggs and bacon. It was the only somewhat enjoyable aspect of the entire trip.

After the meal, Chrissie and her fellow passengers climbed aboard the coach for the final leg of the journey. The five-hour travel was uneventful, even boring, except for the nagging presence of the uncertainty of her father's condition. When the coach pulled up at the depot in Fort Worth, all aboard were ready to get out and stretch their legs.

Fort Worth in 1870 was a one-street town about an eighth of a mile long, with mostly business fronts lining both sides. Residences were dotted around the area in random placement. Commerce was concentrated on Main Street.

While the other passengers would continue on to other locations, Chrissie collected her carpet bag and proceeded to Ed's Livery, where she rented a horse and buggy for the hour-long jaunt to the ranch.

"Bring 'em back when you can, Miss Chrissie," Old Ed told her. "I trusts the Tell."

That was no surprise to Chrissie. Pa always made sure bills were paid on time. No excuses.

She drove the horse gently, recognizing its age, and arrived at the ranch house just after noon. Except for the cook, a crusty, little man in his sixties who wore a patch over a missing eye, the place was deserted.

"They all out to the range."

"And my father?"

"He done went out by his lonesome. Checking on the buffalo calves, he says."

Chrissie knew about Tell's plan to integrate buffalo into the herds. What she didn't know was where on the vast Tell holdings her father might be. "Did he say where?"

"Nope. Didn't say. Could be anywheres."

"Where's Cletus?"

"Took the boys up to the north range today."

Chrissie left the buggy outside the house. After changing into more suitable riding clothes, she pulled on a checkered wool coat and a narrow brimmed canvas hat. She crossed to the barn. There she saddled her pinto mare and struck out to the north at a gallop.

Twenty minutes of sustained riding brought her to the beginning of the north range. The presence of a few stray steers told her she was close to the main herd. She rode through the strays, displacing them, and continued up and over a mild incline. As she descended toward level ground, the main herd and the Tell cowboys became visible directly in front of her. She went on, picking out Cletus from the others, and headed straight for him, now at a gallop.

Her approach was spotted by Terry, who alerted Cletus.

"Cletus." Her call came as he turned his horse to meet her. She pulled up short beside him.

Cletus tipped his hat. "Miss Chrissie." He flashed a smile. "Reckon you got my telly-graph."

Chrissie fought to catch her breath. "I did. You scared the hell out of me."

"Sorry I done that. I ain't so good at writing things, but I needed you to come-a running. It be that important. You seen him yet?"

"No. Cookie says he rode out to check on the buffalo calves."

"Damn! I tried getting him to promise he'd stay home. He should ought to be resting, not riding."

"I know how stubborn he is. Can you break away here and come back to the house with me? You can tell me about Pa on the way."

"Hey, Terry, finish up here, will you? Then head on to the west range. I going back with Miss Chrissie."

Terry waved acknowledgement.

Chrissie turned her horse to side Cletus. They started back to the ranch house. During the ride, Cletus explained what he knew of Tell's ailments. Chrissie's concern for her father grew as she heard more details. The doctor's visit and his secrecy pending his research was the last straw.

"After I talk to Pa, I want to see this doctor. I want to know what he knows. Will you go with me?"

"I surely will."

As they approached the ranch house, Tell stood beside the buggy Chrissie had driven from Fort Worth, looking it over. He held his horse's reins in his hand. The horse grazed behind him.

The sight of her father quickened Chrissie's pace. Her horse was at a trot when she pulled up behind him and dropped from the saddle. "Pa!" She started toward him.

Tell turned, surprised at the call. "Chrissie? Why—? What are you doing home?"

She ran into his arms, embracing him. He responded with a hug of his own.

Chrissie leaned back after a second. "I heard you're sick. I came right away."

"How'd you hear that?"

"Cletus sent me a telegram and asked me to come home."

Chrissie hugged Tell again, but he stiffened. He looked at Cletus as Cletus dismounted nearby.

"What the hell, Cletus? Where do you come off taking liberties like that?"

"You sick enough for the doc to come out. You ain't acting like yourself, or maybe you was. Anyhow, I reckoned Chrissie should ought to know."

Chrissie broke in. "Don't get on Cletus, Pa. He's concerned for you, same as I am. It's right he called me back. You need somebody to keep you from harming yourself."

Tell let out a sigh. "Chrissie, I'm just tired is all. Besides that, I'm all right. You needn't worry yourself." As he spoke, a grimace came over his face.

Chrissie guessed he was in pain. She took charge. "I'll decide that when I know what's ailing you." She turned her father toward the house. "Let's go inside, and you can tell me all about it while you sit down and relax." Her words came out as a gentle order.

Tell dropped the reins and allowed Chrissie to direct him.

"Cletus," he said over his shoulder. "Don't you have things to do?"

Cletus picked up the reins. "Yes, sir."

Tell, slightly hunched over, started walking with Chrissie supporting him. "Then hadn't you better get to 'em?"

"Yes, sir."

Chrissie spent the rest of the afternoon questioning her father.

"You might as well tell me everything, Pa. I can be as cantankerous as you are. You know that."

He related the onslaught of stomach pains and the incident in the Dakotas. She suspected he played down both occurrences as he would normally do with any malady that troubled him. However, she knew him well enough to be certain pressing him further would only cause him to shut down. She would get the truth from the doctor, assuming he had the results of his research. That mission would be embarked upon in the morning.

Chrissie put Tell in his favorite easy chair and set about cooking his favorite dinner, steak and roasted potatoes. It was a quiet meal until Tell sat back, wiping his mouth on his napkin.

"So, will you be heading back to school in the morning?"

"No, Pa. I'm not leaving till I know what's going on with you. You can pass this off as just a belly misery, but I know there's more to it. In the morning, I'm going into Fort Worth to see that doctor. I want to know what he knows."

Tell leaned forward. "Then I'm going with you."

Chrissie shook her head, agitated. "Absolutely not. You need to stay housebound until we know better."

His brow furrowed. "I'm still the parent here—"

"And I'm the daughter who loves you. And if I have to get Cletus to tie you to your bed to keep you safe from yourself, I'll do that."

Tell sat back, cowed by her determination, her stubbornness.

Chrissie saw her father to bed early and then went to her own room. Sleep eluded her that night. The weariness was there, for a fact, but worry kept her tossing and turning until, finally exhausted, she drifted off after midnight.

The light of dawn streaming through her window woke her from her restless slumber. Determined to get to the bottom of this problem, she rose and readied herself for the trip to Fort Worth. Her breakfast was simple. She made certain to make no noise, wanting her father to sleep undisturbed as long as he needed.

As she stepped out onto the porch, her eyes settled on the group of Tell riders standing in front of the barn receiving their instructions for the day from Cletus. She glanced to the right to see the rented buggy parked near the barn door. The absence of the horse told her Cletus had seen to its care, which had escaped her the day before. She stepped off the porch and moved toward the group. "Cletus."

Cletus turned. "Morning, Chrissie."

"Good morning. Are you ready to go to town?" She reached him and stopped. "I've got to talk to that doctor."

"Be right with you." He turned back to the cowboys, addressing Terry. "You running it today. Head 'em out."

Terry nodded and waved the men on. They moved as a group to the corral where their horses waited. In a moment, they were mounted and rode off to the west.

Cletus got the buggy ready while Chrissie saddled her horse. With both their mounts tied behind the carriage, Cletus helped Chrissie aboard and then drove toward the main road.

Their hour long trip to Fort Worth passed in silence. Chrissie contemplated her father's ailments and what she would ask the doctor, chewing her lower lip as she thought. Cletus's stare drew her gaze, and her eyes met his straight on. The concern on his face was evident, both for her and for her father. She tried to force a smile that didn't quite work. Cletus turned away to concentrate on driving.

4

UPON ENTERING THE TOWN, THEY made their first stop at Ed's Livery to return the buggy and pay the rental fee. Old Ed gave them directions to the doctor's office. They mounted their horses and rode the short distance to a storefront that had been converted to house Dr. Ramsey's medical facility. The sign on the double door read *Torben Ramsey, MD*. They dismounted at the hitch rail and tied off their horses.

Cletus went to the door to find it locked. "Ain't here yet."

"Then we'll wait."

They waited a few minutes, during which time Chrissie paced impatiently up and down the boardwalk.

Cletus glanced down the street. "There he be." He pointed to the tall, well-dressed man approaching them.

Chrissie looked in the direction Cletus indicated. She was instantly impressed with the bearing and stature of the man, and she noted he was not much older than she.

Dr. Ramsey walked to them, a smile crossing his face. "Good morning. Cletus, is it not?"

"Yes, sir." Cletus gestured toward Chrissie. "This here's Miss Chrissie Tell."

Ramsey removed his hat and bowed a little at the waist. "It is a pleasure to meet you, Miss Tell."

Keeping her impressions stuffed, Chrissie projected a business-like manner. "How do you do, Doctor. May I speak with you about my father?"

"Of course. Please come inside."

At the office door, Ramsey fished a key from his coat pocket and proceeded to fumble it. His face turned a bit red as he retrieved it from the boardwalk and used it to unlock the office door. He led the way inside. As Chrissie and Cletus stepped into the office, Ramsey hung his hat and coat on a coat tree standing behind the door. He seemed a bit fidgety.

The office consisted of a nondescript wood desk and chair with two wood chairs facing them. Behind the desk, the wall bore the doctor's license framed modestly. To one side, a floor to ceiling bookcase housed volumes of many sizes. All had some medical title. Chrissie recognized some of the words and terms but would have to work at discerning their meanings. Another time perhaps. On the other side, a wood door led to what Chrissie assumed was the examination area.

Ramsey stood behind the desk and focused on Chrissie. He seemed a tad uneasy. "How can I help you?"

"I spent a good part of yesterday with my father, and all I could find out was that he almost froze to death, and he has pains in his stomach. Knowing him as I do, I think he's keeping something from me. I need to know everything you know about his condition."

Ramsey hesitated for a second, letting out a heavy sigh. "Miss Tell, your father is a very ill man. He's developed pneumonia from that freezing incident, but he is recovering slowly from that. Warmer weather should help, although he might have some permanent residual lung damage. However, his stomach pain is more serious. I completed my research last night. Based on my findings and the mass I detected when I examined him, my diagnosis is stomach cancer."

Chrissie was taken aback. She glanced at Cletus as he spoke up. "What's that?"

"Simply put, it's a growth in his stomach. Left untreated, it will increase in size, and the cancer could very well spread to other parts of his body. Eventually, he will succumb."

"Succumb?" Cletus did not know that word.

But Chrissie did. "It means he'll die." She took in a breath to calm herself. "What is the treatment, Doctor?"

"Presently, the only treatment that has shown any positive results at all is one in which an electrical current from storage batteries is used to destroy the growth. However, the success rate is very low. Even at that, I recommend having the procedure. Unfortunately, I do not have the facilities here to perform it. I know of only one place at which it is available, a hospital in Chicago."

Chrissie pondered the information, finding it completely distasteful. "I can only imagine how gruesome that would be. I'll try to convince him to do it, but, honestly, I don't hold out much hope. He's too stubborn."

Ramsey's gaze narrowed on her. "I will, of course, do whatever possible to help him. However, the only course I have open to me is to increase the laudanum dose to make him more comfortable. I must warn you though, laudanum is a very powerful narcotic. In his weakened state, he could become irresponsible and an imminent danger to himself if he is not confined to bed and monitored constantly. As well, I must inform you, his chances for survival are only marginally better with the procedure than without it. Sadly, Miss Tell, I suggest you prepare yourself for the worst."

LATER THE SAME DAY, FURTHER down Main Street, attorney Jarrett Bremmer sat alone in his law office completing the execution of a client's contract. His desk faced the door and was situated in the center of the single, sparsely furnished room. To his right, a floor to ceiling bookcase housed a myriad of law-related volumes. To his left, a wood burning stove stood idle. The cool February weather kept the temperature in the wood frame building low enough to warrant keeping his jacket on instead of working more comfortably in shirt sleeves. A fire in the heater would have warmed the place, but Bremmer's thriftiness precluded that move. He was not about to spend money on firewood and was definitely not going to engage in the physical labor required to chop his own. Wearing the jacket would have to suffice.

Perhaps someday, when his fortunes changed for the better, he would engage in a bit of spending. But not here, not in this one-horse town on the edge of the frontier where charges for services had to be tempered to account for the lack of clients' funds. One couldn't get blood out of the proverbial stone. Someday though, someday he'd have the wherewithal to live a proper life, the life of an attorney whose clients spared no expense in the pursuit of the goals and paid dearly for those services. Not here. San Francisco, perhaps, but not here.

A tall, gaunt man with tiny, beady eyes and a long, prominent nose, Bremmer had a perfectly manicured Van Dyke mustache and beard. He wore a dark blue business suit.

The intricacy of the document on which he worked required him to refer several times for accuracy to the law book that rested in front of him. He was within minutes of finishing the contract when a knock on the door interrupted him, causing him to look up from his work. "Come in." His voice was deep and clear with an oratorical quality.

The door opened to admit Bruno Tell. He wore more clothing than Bremmer thought necessary, a heavy, plaid wool coat and a wool scarf adjusted tightly about his neck. Bremmer recognized his visitor immediately, having had dealings with Tell in the past. And that weathered face and lanky figure were hard to forget. Even one meeting left a lasting impression.

"Mister Tell, good day to you. What can I do for you?" As Bremmer spoke the greeting, he noticed something odd about Tell. The sour look on his face and the way he carried himself, slightly bent, he looked elderly or even wounded. Bremmer was familiar enough with Tell's manner to notice this was not normal for him. There was also that distant look in Tell's eyes, as if he'd had a few. Bremmer was intrigued.

"Bremmer," Tell said in greeting. He moved forward, closing the door behind him, and stopped at the desk. "I need your help." Tell's voice was shaky, not his usual, commanding tone. He spoke slowly and seemed to have difficulty forming the words.

Further captivated by this anomaly, Bremmer engaged with his guest. "Of course, of course. Please, have a seat."

Tell took a seat in the wooden chair facing the desk. He let out a loud breath, almost a wince, as he sat down. Bremmer picked up on the discomfort Tell's expression and demeanor conveyed.

"What assistance can I provide?" Bremmer sounded rather formal.

"I need to make some provisions for my daughter to be taken care of and to secure the future of my ranch." Tell loosened his scarf and opened his coat. "I need it all written down legally, and I need it done fast. I think I'm dying."

Now Bremmer was completely drawn in. Besides being excited

by the anticipation of the fee this would bring him, he was surprised by Tell's revelation. He leaned forward in a solicitous way. "Mister Tell, I will, of course, help in any way possible, but are you certain of what you say?"

Tell nodded. "Certain enough to realize this is something I should've done long ago. I just hope I'm not too late to secure Chrissie's future now."

"How... how much time... before—"

Tell cut him off, shaking his head. "No idea."

Bremmer picked up his pencil and pulled a blank sheet of paper in front of him. "Well, whatever you want done, you have but to tell me. I'll make this a priority and draft a document straight away. Once it's signed and recorded, it will be legal and binding. You have my assurance on that." As he spoke, Bremmer's mind wandered, settling on what possibilities might lie ahead if he had complete control over the future of this man's holdings after his death. He fought back a smile of anticipation.

"Then let's get to it." Tell explained that he wanted a trust set up for Chrissie that would create an account separate from the ranch's business account. He designated an amount that would be deposited monthly into that account from the profits of the ranch operations. From that, Chrissie would receive a monthly allowance until she reached the age of twenty-five. Since the cost of her education was already paid for, this money would sustain Chrissie until such time as she either married or became self-sufficient.

Bremmer wrote furiously to keep up with Tell's instructions.

Tell continued. "I know the law doesn't permit minors to own property without oversight. So, after I'm gone, the operation of the Tell will be controlled by the bank. They'll run the spread and ensure it stays profitable. I want you to become Chrissie's guardian until she comes of age and to see that the bank carries out the ranch operation properly."

Bremmer looked up from his writing. "Mister Tell, is there no one else who can assume that responsibility? A relative, perhaps?"

"There's no one. The only other man I'd trust to protect Chrissie and her interests is my foreman, Cletus Workman. But I'm aware that his being a Negro would present serious problems with that. That's why I'm asking you to do it. I will stipulate though that I want Cletus kept on as foreman. I want that in your writing. He knows the Tell, he's loyal to me, and he thinks of Chrissie as his own, so he'll watch everything real careful. I guarantee you'll hear from him if things aren't right. You won't want to get on his bad side."

"Mister Tell, I assure you, I would ne—"

Tell cut him off in mid-sentence. "I'm just telling you Cletus'll see that nothing goes wrong. Now, you'll get a monthly fee for your part in this, one we can both agree on. Same with the bank. Can I count on you?"

Bremmer nodded without hesitation. "Absolutely."

"Then finish it up, and let's make it legal."

Bremmer continued writing. It took a half hour for him to complete the transcription. He looked up from his work as he put down the pencil. "I can't speak to the bank's requirements or its participation. We'll need to continue this discussion with Mister Manion included."

"We can go over there right now. I want this agreed upon today." Tell stood up, supporting himself on the desk, and buttoned his coat.

Bremmer rose. "Very well." He collected the paperwork and rounded the desk to get his homburg hat from the hat tree near the door.

Together, they left the office and crossed the street diagonally toward a small wood building with a tall facade bearing the designation, *Seal and Manion Savings and Loan Assn.*

Tell seemed unstable on his feet. Bremmer had to slow down to allow Tell to catch up. Traffic in the street was forced to stop or go around to avoid colliding with the two men.

Tell and Bremmer entered the bank, a small building with a wire enclosure along three quarters of the back wall. Inside it, a floor to ceiling vault stood in one corner. The rest of the space was occupied by file cabinets. A teller sat on a stool at an opening in the enclosed space. From there he serviced customers' deposits and withdrawals.

Bremmer led the way to the door at the back that completed the final quarter of the wall. He knocked and waited. As Tell joined him, a voice called permission to enter from the other side. Bremmer went in. Tell followed.

Inside, the room was long and narrow, filling the full width of the rear of the building. A door to the back alley and a window immediately adjacent to it faced them as they walked in. To their right, a long, overstuffed couch sat against the back wall. Beyond that, in the center of the right corner, facing them, a polished wooden desk was situated. There were matching guest chairs in front of it.

At the desk, a stocky man with a full beard rose as they entered. He was slightly taller than medium height with a full head of dark, silver-streaked hair. His beard was varying shades of gray. He was dressed in an expensive wool suit, brocade vest, and a dark cravat. The nameplate on the desk read *Vincent Manion, Pres.*

"Good day, gentlemen." His voice was deep, gravelly. "Why, Mister Tell, it's been quite some time since you paid us a visit. How are things?"

Manion's expression betrayed his apparent notice of Tell's ailing look. Bremmer silently took that in.

"Mister Manion," Tell said in greeting. "Things are not good. I—we need your help."

"That sounds serious." Manion gestured to the guest chairs. "Please, sit down."

Tell and Bremmer took seats.

Manion sat down. "What can I do for you?"

Bremmer handed over the papers. "I think the easiest way to explain this would be for you to look this over. This is the draft of a document Mister Tell has asked me to compose for him. It involves the participation of the bank."

Manion took the sheets and began reading. His expression changed several times as he progressed through it. He registered first interest, then surprise, then concern. He looked past the papers at Tell. "Do I understand this to indicate... you're not well?"

"I'm dying, Manion." Tell leaned forward in the chair. "I don't know what it is, but it's killing me. I can feel it coming. Keeps getting worse. Chrissie's all I got. I want to make sure she's set before I pass. I've taken steps to ensure the value of the Tell herd by integrating buffalo into it for strength. In a year or two, the value of the herd should double. Run right, the Tell can live on into the future and support Chrissie. I'm here now to see that what we do today insures that."

Manion handed the draft back to Bremmer and spoke to Tell. "The bank will cooperate fully. We want to help you in your planning. I can't tell you how sorry I am that this has come about."

Tell breathed a sigh. "Yeah, well, it is what it is. I guess it's just my time."

Seconds of an awkward silence ticked by until Bremmer spoke up. "Well, it would seem we only have to agree on the fees for the bank and for my services. Once that's in place, I can finalize the agreement, and we can put things in motion."

Tell leaned back. "I was thinking two hundred a month each would be acceptable."

Bremmer spoke right up. "Fine with me. Manion?"

Manion remained silent, thinking.

Bremmer chided him. "Come on, Manion. The man is clearly in difficulty here. You said you wanted to help."

"Well, yes, I suppose I can live with that. Yes, of course."

Tell smiled. "Thank you, gentlemen." He appeared relieved.

Bremmer turned to Tell. "I'll write this up properly and bring it out to the ranch tonight for your signature."

Tell got up but faltered, grabbing the desk to support and balance himself. "Damn laudanum. Hate the stuff, but it does work for the pain." Now stabilized, he started for the door.

Bremmer called after him, "Take care."

"I'm trying," Tell said as he opened the door and went out.

As the door closed, Bremmer turned back to Manion. "So, Manion, do you see what I see here?"

Manion nodded. "Yes, I see a very desperate man."

Bremmer shook his head. "I see much more than that. I see an opportunity. A big one."

"An opportunity?" Manion thought for a moment. "I'm sure I don't see—"

"Come on, man, use your head. Tell dies, and we're in control of the richest spread in east Texas. If this is handled correctly, it'll make us both rich."

Manion's face finally registered awareness. "Oh... oh... I see."

"Well, it took you long enough."

Manion seemed shocked. "But that's not... not ethical, not—"

Bremmer pushed harder. "Are you seriously concerned with ethics? Out here on the edge of nowhere? This is not San Francisco."

Manion became quiet as he pondered the prospect. "I don't know, Bremmer. What about his daughter... and the foreman. That document specifically mentions the foreman. It's risky. If we're found out, we'll—"

"We won't be found out. Besides, we'll have the law on our side. You let me worry about the details and the legalities. Slowly but surely we'll do away with any interference the girl or the foreman can offer. All we have to do is wait."

"I don't know. It could take years."

"Did you get a good look at him? He's half dead now." Bremmer pointed toward the door and shook his finger. "Even if it does take years, we're still getting paid to wait. Look, a chance like this comes once in a lifetime. We need to grab it. Now."

Manion was silent.

Bremmer did not let up. "Do you want to do this for the rest of your life, handle other people's money and get only a small fraction of it? Or do you want it to be your own money? I know what I want, and it's not just scratching out a living the way I am now. I want more, much more, and I don't care how I get it. What about you?"

"Of course I do, but there are so many ways this could go wrong. That black foreman worries me."

Bremmer held the draft up in front of Manion. "You worry too much, Manion. All you need to do is run the ranch. I'll handle the nigga. He won't be a problem, but this won't work if you're not in."

Manion breathed a heavy sigh. "Well, all right. What do you need me to do?"

"For now, set up the trust for the girl and arrange the plans to assume control of the ranch after Tell's gone. I'll take care of every-thing else. Just remember one thing. You commit to this, there's no going back. We see this through to the end, no matter what it takes, or it's dead before it begins. It becomes just another legal arrange-ment, and we get nothing but that meager fee."

"I understand."

Bremmer nodded. "I hope you do."

5

ETURNING FROM FORT WORTH DURING late morning, Chrissie and Cletus entered the main area of the Tell and proceeded to the hitch rail in front of the ranch house porch. Predictably, the area was deserted except for the smoke spilling from the stovepipe affixed to the cook shack.

Chrissie dismounted and stepped onto the porch. Cletus took up the reins to Chrissie's horse and led it toward the barn as Chrissie stepped inside the house. She went to the coat tree to hang up her coat and found the rack empty. Wondering where her father's coat and hat were, she hurried up the stairs to the second floor and stopped at the door to his bedroom. She knocked. No answer came. Again she knocked, louder this time, on the chance that he was sleeping. Still no reply.

Now concerned, she turned the knob and opened the door. The bed was unmade and unoccupied. Where was he?

"Pa?" Her call was loud enough to be heard throughout the house. She was sure of that. Her answer was silence.

Oh, God, what if he had another attack? He'd be alone out there. Concern turned to alarm. She ran out of the room and bounded down the stairs, stopping on the porch to call again. Her voice echoed against the buildings and brought Cletus out of the barn. He stopped short in the doorway.

"Pa's gone."

As her voice echoed again, Cookie opened the door of the cook shack and stepped out.

Chrissie heard the sound and turned to him. "Cookie, where's my father?"

"He done went to town, Miss Chrissie. Headed out a tad after you and Cletus left. Ain't come back since."

"Did he say why he went?"

"No, ma'am, just he was a-going."

Chrissie sucked in a breath. Panic took hold. She stepped off the porch and trotted across the yard toward the barn. Reaching where Cletus stood, she brushed past him. "I've got to find him."

Cletus followed her into the barn as she reached her horse. "You got no idea where he be."

"I don't care." She led the unsaddled horse out of the stall. "I'll take the trail he always takes. If I don't find him there, I'll search the whole of Fort Worth if I have to."

"You ain't doing that on your lonesome. I'll side you."

They saddled up again and headed out with Chrissie in the lead at a gallop. As soon as they reached the trail Tell was known to follow to Fort Worth, they slowed and scanned the area in front of them as they rode. They found nothing.

Chrissie's mind went in all directions. This situation would not have reached the proportions it had if she'd been home. She would have seen the signs sooner, and maybe could have done something, but she didn't know what. She understood Pa's reasoning for sending her to Charnwood, but school would have to wait. How long, she didn't know. But there was really no hurry. It could be done at any time. Yes, it was important, but the most important thing in Chrissie's life right now was her father. Where was he, anyway?

Cletus tried to read signs as they rode, but the ground was too rocky to make out anything meaningful. A few strikes on some of the stones could have been made by horseshoes, but who they belonged to and how old they were could not be determined. They followed the route for close to a half hour to no avail. Chrissie became more frustrated and worried with each passing minute.

Cresting a hill, they started down the slope toward level ground. The height of the knoll allowed an almost panoramic view of the area for at least a mile. Chrissie pulled up short. "Cletus, look." She pointed to a distant outline resembling a horse and rider coming toward them at a very slow pace.

"I see 'em. They too far. Can't be sure."

Chrissie slapped the reins across her horse's hindquarters, generating an immediate gallop. "Come on."

Cletus fell in behind her. They finished the descent at a dangerous pace. As they scrambled across flatter country, the image became clearer. The rider was doubled over the horse's neck. As they drew closer, they could make out the clothes, the familiar hat and coat. Chrissie was certain it was her father.

With her heart pounding heavily, Chrissie urged her horse to a greater speed. Cletus caught up with her and touched her arm to get her attention.

"Slow down. You'll spook him."

Chrissie realized that charging at the animal might well cause it to panic and run. She pulled her horse back to a trot and allowed Cletus to take the lead and proceed slowly. Aware that the horse was more familiar with Cletus, she dropped back and deferred to Cletus's expertise.

He approached the mount, speaking low, calming words. This allowed him to come alongside and take the reins from Tell's grip. Chrissie rode up and stopped.

Leaning forward, Cletus lifted Tell from his position around the horse's neck. Chrissie moved in closer to see her father struggling to stay conscious, a battle he was losing.

Cletus placed Tell back into the position on the horse's neck. "We got to get him home." Dismounting, he handed his reins to Chrissie. "You lead my horse back. I'll ride with Mister Tell and see he don't fall off." He stepped up onto Tell's horse, sitting behind Tell. He placed his arms under Tell's arms to hold Tell upright and then directed the horse forward. They backtracked toward the ranch at a slow pace.

CLETUS DESCENDED THE STAIRS TO the first floor of the ranch house. Chrissie paced about the foyer nervously, tearfully, deeply entrenched in her worries about her father.

"He safe in bed," Cletus said.

Chrissie turned and focused on her black friend, wiping away her tears with the back of her hand. "Cletus, I don't know where I'd be if you weren't here."

"Well, you ain't got to find that out, Miss Chrissie, 'cause I ain't going nowheres. You want I should fetch that doc?"

"No. It's useless. He can't do anything. He said it himself. All he can do is increase the laudanum. Hell, I can do that. What I can't do is convince Pa to have the operation. He's too damn stubborn for his own good." She turned away to hide her tears.

Cletus placed his hand on her arm to comfort him. She turned and fell into his arms, sobbing. He pulled her close.

"Aw, Chrissie, I sorely hates you gots to be saddened like this."

Chrissie hugged Cletus tighter, then leaned back. "I'm not giving up. I'm going to keep trying to talk him into it. Is he awake now?"

Cletus shook his head. "Naw, he sleeping sound."

"I'll try again when he wakes up. Did he say anything, anything about why he went to town?"

"He rambled on a mite, but none of it made no sense. I reckon he just wore out. Needs to rest up."

Chrissie turned toward the kitchen. "I'll make some soup to give him later. I've got to keep busy."

"I savvy that. Look, I got to go check on the boys. They out on the west range. You need me, you send Cookie out there fetching me. I'll come a-running."

"All right, I will." Chrissie went into the kitchen as Cletus left the house.

For the next few hours, Chrissie made soup, Pa's favorite soup. While she could have easily requested Cookie to do the job, the point of this exercise was to busy herself to keep her father's condition from driving her crazy. It would also provide her the chance to make something of her own for him, like she did when she was little. After Ma died, Pa never let her do much around the ranch. Losing Ma made him twice as protective of her. But she could make soup. And that satisfied her need to help. Today it would be therapeutic. She obtained cooked chicken parts from the cook shack and began cutting and chopping the meat and some vegetables.

Peeling and cutting onions drew tears, and that pushed her over the edge. She stopped and succumbed to the feeling of remorse and the fear of loss, pulling her apron up over her face to cry and release her emotions.

After a few moments, she regained her composure and wiped

the tears from her face with the apron. She had to keep it together. Taking care of Pa was more important than giving in to her feelings. Pulling in a deep cleansing breath, she went back to work, adding the ingredients to a pot of boiling water. Damn it, she'd make this soup.

She proceeded steadily, only stopping periodically to check on Tell. Each time she found him fast asleep. This she attributed to the exhaustion the Fort Worth trip had no doubt caused him.

As the soup was in its final minutes of preparation, Chrissie climbed the stairs to the second floor once more. She tapped her knuckles softly on the bedroom door and waited.

"Come in." Tell's voice was weak and seemed distant to Chrissie. She opened the door and stepped in.

Tell looked up from his attempt to pull himself to a sitting position in the bed. Chrissie moved to the bed to help. She slid her arm under Tell's and pulled him up. He grunted as he moved. He might have been weak as a kitten, but he was still a big man. Together they managed to get him to where he wanted to be. She leaned closer to him, stooping at the waist.

"Chrissie, what're you still doing here? You should be in school. Your studies are going to slip."

"I've only been home for a day, Pa."

He looked away, giving her the impression he was struggling to piece things together, maybe trying to remember and failing at it. After a few seconds, he looked at her again. "Oh, yeah, yeah. Seemed like longer, I guess." Still, he had that distant look in his eyes.

Chrissie made the assumption that the laudanum was dulling his senses in its efforts to quell the pain, maybe affecting his memory. "Pa, how do you feel?"

He looked away again. This time Chrissie guessed he was assessing himself. He turned back to her.

"Tired. Real tired. Gnawing in my gut. Guess that stuff's working." He gestured to the vial on the night table. "Pain's mostly gone."

She laid her hand on his forehead. He felt warm. "Do you feel like eating something? I made soup."

A wan smile crossed his face. He nodded. "Yeah, that sounds real good, girl."

Chrissie went back downstairs and filled a bowl with soup. She placed a spoon in the bowl and, holding it with her apron, walked it carefully to Tell's bedside. Running through her mind was the distinct possibility that this could be the last time she'd make this soup for him. She shuddered at the thought, but in her heart she knew....

She spoon-fed him until he indicated he'd had enough, then put the bowl aside.

"I spoke to Doctor Ramsey this morning." She looked straight ahead, not at her father.

"Yeah, he was here. Said he needed to research this thing, whatever it is, before he put a name to it." He seemed more alert now. Maybe the soup did the trick. "What'd he say to you?"

She took in a sharp breath and exhaled. "He said you have a cancer in your stomach." She had to force the words out.

"He say what that is?"

Chrissie turned her gaze to her father. "It's a growth that just keeps getting bigger." Tears welled up in her eyes. Her face contorted in distress. "Pa, you could die." She lost what little control she'd had, throwing her arms around him in a desperate embrace.

"I know that, Chrissie." He spoke quietly, perceptively, as she sobbed into his shoulder. His arms enveloped her weakly. "I can feel it coming for me."

Chrissie lifted her head from his shoulder and wiped her tears away. "Pa, listen to me, please. Doctor Ramsey told me there's a treatment, a procedure that might be able to help you. You'd have to go to Chicago for it. That's the only place they do it, but it's something. It's something. You wouldn't have to just... accept that you're going to die."

"And what is this treatment he told you about? What're they going to do, cut this thing out of me?"

"He said they use wires and electric batteries."

"I got no idea what those things do, but let me tell you something. I been shot and stabbed and damn near trampled in my lifetime. I'll never allow anybody to cut on me or wire me up or anything like that. None of that's natural. I won't have it. You hear me? I won't have it."

"But, Pa—"

"Chrissie, you listen here. My time is nigh. Nothing's going to change that. You'd best prepare yourself for it. I love you, girl, but you're not little anymore. You're old enough now to understand this and accept it. If I got to go, it's going to be on my terms, making things right for you, for your future, making sure the Tell lives on for you. I set my mind to that. Don't try to change it."

Still sobbing, Chrissie laid her head on his shoulder again. "I only want what's best for you, Pa."

He stroked her back. "I know, Chrissie, I know. But you got to allow that it's my choice, my decision. You got to let it go."

They remained in that position, while Chrissie regained her composure. Tell advised her that he needed to rest again. She stood up and helped him to lie down, then she pulled the covers up on him. As he closed his eyes, Chrissie picked up the soup bowl and left the room, making sure she left the door open. She wanted to be able to hear anything emanating from the room and provide herself quick access to it.

Toward evening, Chrissie responded to a knock on the front door. She opened it to a tall man in business attire, clutching a brief-case under his arm. He removed his hat and smiled.

"Good evening. Miss Tell?"

Chrissie's formal manners engaged immediately. "I am, but I'm afraid you have me at a disadvantage, sir."

"My apologies. My name is Jarrett Bremmer. I'm your father's attorney. May I speak with him?"

"He's resting now. He's actually quite ill and really shouldn't be disturbed. Can this wait?"

Bremmer took a step closer. "Miss Tell, he was quite emphatic when we met this morning that he wanted me to bring these papers for his signature as soon as possible. I'm merely following his instructions."

Chrissie fidgeted, trying to do the right thing. "Well, I'm—"

"Chrissie!" Tell's voice reached her ears, interrupting her. "It's all right. Let him in."

She weighed her options. Her first instinct was to keep her father from any activity. His voice, however, sounded both insistent and a bit stronger. She allowed that a few minutes should not cause any harm. She stepped aside.

Bremmer moved inside and stopped.

"His room is at the top of the stairs." Chrissie closed the front door. "Please be brief."

"Thank you. I'm well aware of his weakened condition. I promise I won't overtax him." Bremmer went up the steps and into Tell's room.

Chrissie glanced upstairs to see the door closing. Voices came from inside the room, but they were muffled, preventing her from understanding the words. Realizing it was improper to listen, she went into the kitchen to busy herself there.

Only a few minutes passed. Chrissie heard Bremmer call her

name. She went into the foyer to find him near the door. She approached him.

"My business with Mister Tell is finished. It was a great pleasure meeting you. Again, my apologies for barging in like this. I'll be leaving now."

"It's all right. You needn't apologize." Chrissie opened the door for him. "I understand how insistent my father can be. Goodbye, Mister Bremmer."

"Miss Tell." Bremmer stepped out and, putting his hat on, went to his horse at the hitch rail.

Chrissie watched him mount and leave, wondering about the nature of this business he had with her father. Obviously, Pa wanted this kept secret, or he would have enlightened her. She would respect his wishes.

6

BREMMER SAT IN MANION'S OFFICE a few days later. It was morning. The winter cold began giving way to a burgeoning spring and warmer temperatures, but Bremmer still wore his overcoat. With his hat perched on his knee, he opened the briefcase on his lap and extracted some papers.

The door from the bank opened to admit Manion. He stopped in his tracks at the sight of Bremmer.

"Morning, Manion," Bremmer said offhandedly.

"How did you get in here?" Manion's voice was demanding.

Bremmer smiled without looking up. He continued shuffling through the papers. "Relax. I just told your teller I had business with you. He let me in."

"I'll have to have a talk with him." Manion crossed to the desk. "I can't have just anyone walking in here when I'm not present."

"I'm not just anyone. I'm your partner. The sooner you get used to that, the better."

Manion grumbled. He reached into his vest pocket and brought out a key. "All right, but next time use the back door. This key will unlock it." He moved closer to Bremmer and handed over the key. "The less we're seen together, the better."

Bremmer pocketed the object. "All right, fine, you've asserted yourself. Now, sit down. I've got something to show you."

Manion took off his coat and hung it and his hat on the wall-mounted hook behind the desk. As he took his seat, Bremmer handed him a set of papers.

"Read that over."

Manion skimmed the document and put it aside.

Bremmer gave him another set. "Now read this."

Dutifully, Manion perused again.

Bremmer leaned in. "Notice anything different?"

Manion looked at him quizzically, unable to answer. He picked up the documents and went over them again, this time more carefully. "There's no mention of the foreman in this one."

"Exactly."

"How did you...?"

"Easy. I had Tell read and sign the original containing the passage about the foreman, then I gave him what I passed off as copies. He never read the copies. He simply signed them. This eliminates any threat the foreman could pose. As soon as we take over, he'll be gone."

"But what about the original?"

"Burn it. It will have never existed. If you go over them more carefully, you'll find the copy also gives us more latitude than the original. As soon as Tell dies, we'll be right where we need to be."

"I hope you know what you're doing." Manion looked away, concerned. "I'm not so certain."

Bremmer saw Manion's resolve wavering again. He had to put a stop to it. "Look, Manion, the only reason you're in this is because Tell brought the bank into it. If I could have done this on my own, I would have. But, make no mistake, you are in it. Now, before we go any further, burn that original."

Manion hesitated, gazing at the papers. He seemed not all there. Bremmer cleared his throat loudly to bring Manion back from where he'd drifted. It worked. Manion picked up and deposited the original document into the metal waste basket next to his desk. He produced a match from his vest pocket, struck it, and dropped it in, appearing to speed up the process to get it over with. The paper flared up and burned down to a few cinders.

Bremmer sat back. "Well, now you're really in this. You just destroyed evidence."

With suddenness, Manion's face displayed his realization that he'd just been duped. "Bremmer, you son of—"

"Oh, shut up, Manion. Now we're equally guilty. Neither of us can testify against the other with impunity. The perfect partnership."

"Was that really necessary?"

"Based on your attitude, yes, it was. But it's done now. From here on, we share equally in the profits. All we have to do is wait for Tell to die. From the look of him when I was there, we won't have long to wait."

FOR THE NEXT WEEK, CHRISSIE remained at home. Her studies were relegated to the background as she took over caring for her father as well as resuming the domestic duties she'd been in charge of before leaving for school. As his caretaker, Chrissie restricted Tell's activities to prevent sapping what little strength he had left. He grumbled, but he allowed it.

For his part, Cletus took on whatever responsibilities Tell could not discharge. He involved his boss only when doing so became absolutely unavoidable. At one point, Cletus tried to convince Tell to have the operation. He was rebuffed in the same manner as Chrissie had been earlier.

In the kitchen one evening near the end of that week, Chrissie finished washing the dinner dishes. A thump sounded through the ceiling from the location of her father's room. Hastily drying her hands on her apron as she moved, Chrissie hurried from the kitchen, up the stairs, and into the bedroom. She had long since given up knocking on the door before entering. As she cleared the doorway, Tell lay face down on the floor beside the bed. She rushed to him and crouched. "Pa!"

Tell did not react, nor did he move.

A chill ran down Chrissie's spine. Shuddering, she laid a hand on his shoulder. *Oh, God, he's done it. He's left me all alone.* No. Cletus. She wasn't alone. The thought ran through her mind as she bounded out of the room and down the stairs. She crossed to the front door and yanked it open. "Cletus!" Her voice was at scream level as she ran into the yard. She called Cletus's name over and over.

Responding to Chrissie's cries, Cletus came out of the bunkhouse, pulling his suspenders up, and hurried toward her.

"It's Pa." She pointed toward the house. Although Cletus was right there, the feeling of aloneness gripped her again. She took a breath, shuddering.

Cletus ran to her, then stopped. Their eyes met as he seemed to read her mind. He nodded, then ran past her and into the house as Chrissie began breaking down in tears. The Tell hands, led by Terry and Cookie, came out of the bunkhouse to crowd around Chrissie.

Tense moments later, Cletus emerged from the house slowly, his head hung down. He approached the group, pushed his way through the men, making his way to Chrissie, shaking his head. "He gone." Cletus's voice cracked as he spoke.

For a moment, Chrissie just stared at him in disbelief. Oh, God, it's true. It wasn't a dream. It happened. He was gone, gone for good. Then she succumbed to deep grief, falling into Cletus's arms. He embraced her as she surrendered to hysteria, sobbing into his chest.

The hands became quiet as the news took hold. Terry looked away. Cookie sniffed back a tear and scratched at his nose. Chrissie blocked out their presence, consumed by her grief and the consolation provided by Cletus, while Cletus concentrated on calming her. That effort took several minutes, during which the cowboys milled around nearby, discussing the event in whispers.

Finally, Cletus turned to them as Chrissie stepped back from his arms. "Terry, you and the boys see to Mister Tell, will you? We got to take him to town."

Terry reacted silently, gesturing to the others to follow him to a point a few yards away. There he assigned different tasks to them, dispatching several to collect the body from the house and others to hitch up and prepare a buckboard for the trip to Fort Worth.

At a distance, Chrissie caught some of this, but her mind deflected it. She allowed Cletus to usher her around to the rear of the barn, knowing his intention was to shield her from the sight of her father's body being moved. By now, she welcomed the distance. She'd seen enough.

The cowboys worked fast. In the space of a short time, they had wrapped Tell's body in a blanket and brought it to the yard. They placed it gently, reverently, into the bed of the waiting buckboard. From behind the barn, Cletus watched their progress. When they had finished, he collected Chrissie and brought her to the yard as the hands saddled their horses. They mounted as Cletus helped Chrissie onto the buckboard seat, shielding her from viewing the body, and climbed to take the seat beside her.

He raised a halting hand to Terry. "No. Ain't no need you fellows coming along,"

Terry took a breath. "Yeah, Cletus, there's need."

Cookie chimed in. "Mighty well told, Terry." His voice cracked with emotion.

The cowboys fell in behind the buckboard. Cletus slapped the reins across the team's backs and called out to them. The party moved out slowly.

Following a protracted, reflective trip to Fort Worth that ended well after dark, they roused the undertaker from his after-dinner relaxation and turned Tell's body over to him. He informed them that arrangements would consume the next day, and the funeral would be conducted the morning after that. Chrissie found the composure required to give him the location of the funeral, the small family graveyard on the west range of the Tell.

Early on the morning of the funeral, Chrissie put on the clothes she'd laid the day before. She joined Cletus and the hands in the yard, noting that they had donned their newest, cleanest clothing for the occasion. Cletus wore a dark suit, a tad threadbare in spots. Terry wore a collarless white shirt, buttoned to the neck. Cookie had a pin-striped jacket on over a newer striped shirt and a black derby hat.

As she strode toward them, forcing her head high, Chrissie reviewed the previous day. After a restless, sleepless night, still exhausted, she went through her closet for clothing suitable to wear for the funeral. Her heart was not in this. She wanted it all to just go away, but she was Bruno Tell's daughter. As such, she was enough of a realist to know she had to see this through. She owed it to him to honor him in death as she had in life. Settling on a dark, subdued style dress, she put the garment aside and laid out the rest of her outfit—hat, gloves, and coat—to be ready for the ordeal to come.

Having eaten nothing all day, Chrissie was persuaded by Cletus to join the crew in the cook shack for supper. While she ate very little, she welcomed the company and support of the Tell riders. She was not disappointed. They crowded around her and tried their best to cheer her up, telling stories of the early days of the ranch and Tell's exploits to make a safe haven for those who, like him, wanted no part of what Cookie termed "the recent conflict." Chrissie learned more of the stalwart individual Tell was and the lengths to which he'd gone to protect the sanctity of the Tell.

At the end of the evening, as exhaustion took its toll, Chrissie bid the boys goodnight. As she cleared the bunkhouse door, Cletus followed her out.

"Chrissie, I gots to say something."

She turned to face him.

"Don't know if'n it's the right time, but I know your pa'd want you to go back to that school and finish. When this bad time is behind you, there be no need for you to stay on here. You leave the Tell running to me. I'll see to it. You knows that, don't you?"

Chrissie's smile was warm. "I know that, Cletus. But this has all been so much. I can't see beyond today. My mind is too clouded to think clearly. I'll make that decision when I'm able."

Cletus nodded. "I savvy that. I'm just saying what I know your pa'd want, but I'll back you, whatever you decide. That's a promise."

Chrissie wiped an errant tear away. "Thank you, Cletus. That means more to me than I can say." She squeezed out a smile. "You have a good night."

"You as well."

As Chrissie joined the group, Cletus assigned a few of the newer cowboys to handle ranch chores, as they didn't know Tell as well as the others, and somebody had to see to the herd.

The buggy was brought out of the barn hitched and ready. Cletus helped Chrissie aboard, and the trip to Fort Worth was begun.

At the undertaker's establishment, Chrissie watched in despair as the plain wooden coffin containing her father's remains was placed into the hearse. The undertaker, dressed in his mourning coat and high silk hat, drove the enclosed black wagon at a walk, leading the procession on the journey to the west range of the Tell. As they entered the area, they moved to the location of the gravesite. Set between two cottonwood trees, it bore the marker of the grave of Chrissie's mother, Selena, who had died a few years after Chrissie's birth.

Chrissie's memories of her mother were scant. She knew the woman for only five years. The recollections were episodic at best, mostly of her beauty and her caring nature, but nothing specific. Chrissie noted the dates carved on the marker. *Born 1832. Died 1855.* She couldn't call to mind the cause of her mother's demise. She'd have to ask. Oh, God, she couldn't ask Pa. Not about that—or anything else, ever again.

Cletus's hand on Chrissie's arm brought her back to reality. He had pulled the buggy horse to a stop and now told her she needed to get down. With his assistance, she climbed down and approached the newly opened grave next to her mother's.

Terry and three Tell riders pulled the casket from the hearse and shouldered it. With quiet respect, they walked it to the gravesite and placed it on two stout planks that lay across the opening. Two lengths of rope also stretched across the hole. They stepped back as the undertaker moved to the head of the grave. Chrissie and Cletus joined them.

The undertaker read the twenty-third psalm from the Bible he carried and then led the party in reciting the Lord's Prayer. He directed the cowboys to suspend the coffin by means of the ropes, while two other men removed the boards. Then he asked them to lower the casket into the grave. When it was seated at the bottom, each participant dropped a handful of earth in after it.

Chrissie's attempt resulted in her near collapse as the realization of her father's passing took final hold. Cletus supported her as she dropped the dirt in. She fell sobbing into his arms. He walked her toward the buggy. As he started helping her onto the seat, Terry's voice behind them sounded cryptic. "Cletus."

Cletus stopped. He looked in the direction Terry pointed. Chrissie followed suit, becoming engaged in the sight. A group of mounted men had gathered on a knoll a short distance away. Two were well dressed while the other four behind them were in trail clothes.

"What do you make of them?" Terry asked.

Cletus shrugged. "I don't know. Maybe they didn't want to horn in on us."

Chrissie studied the group. "I recognize the one on the left. He's Pa's lawyer."

"Yeah, that's likely it. Hanging back till we leave. Let's get you to home." Cletus finished getting Chrissie into the buggy and climbed in beside her. They took the lead and were followed by the Tell hands as they left the area.

After traveling half a mile, Terry looked over his shoulder to see the group of six riding behind them a few hundred feet. "Them rannies is tailing us."

"Leave it be, Terry. We got other things to see to." Cletus snapped up the buggy horse to increase the pace.

They continued at that rate until they reached the ranch house. The party behind them maintained the same speed and followed them to the edge of the area. As Cletus helped Chrissie from the buggy, the cowboys dismounted. Bremmer led his group forward, stopping them a few yards away. They remained mounted while he got down and approached Chrissie.

Cletus stepped between them. "Help you?"

Bremmer paid the black man no heed. He continued to within three feet of Chrissie and stopped. "Miss Tell, please allow me to offer my sincerest condolences on the passing of your father. Such a tragedy."

Chrissie showed no reaction.

Bremmer continued. "My apologies for any inconvenience this causes, but there is pressing business we must conclude immediately."

Cletus stepped in front of Bremmer. "Miss Tell just buried her father, mister. Any business you got with her can wait a spell."

"What I have to say is quite important, so you just back away, boy." Bremmer stared at him, disdain in his voice and on his face.

Cletus's reaction was swift. "You don't call me boy. I a free man, same as you."

Calmed to the point that her presence of mind had returned, Chrissie saw this getting out of hand. "It's all right, Cletus. I'll listen to what Mister Bremmer has to say."

Cletus nodded and stepped aside.

Bremmer reached inside his coat and brought out a folded pack of papers. "Miss Tell, this is the document your father charged me to write and record. This copy is yours, which you can read over at your leisure. Since its provisions take effect immediately, I'll summarize it for you. Upon his demise, Mister Tell has appointed me as your legal guardian until you reach the age of twenty-one. He has also assigned the operation of the Tell Ranch to the Seal and Manion Savings and Loan Association, under the direction of Mister Manion there." Bremmer indicated Manion, who was still mounted. "Those are the general provisions. When you're feeling better, I can answer any questions you might have before you return to your school. However, there are stipulations that Mister Manion will need to institute straight away to insure the proper workings of the ranch. I'll let him enumerate those."

Chrissie took the document from Bremmer's extended hand and stood staring at it. She opened it to the last page to see her father's signature affixed to it. Making no comment, she looked at Cletus. She read the confusion on his face, the same look she was certain appeared on her own. What had Pa done? Why?

Manion interrupted Chrissie's muddled thoughts. "Miss Tell, my condolences as well. Now, in order to operate the ranch at its most efficient, I need to make some changes. First of all, and mind you, there is nothing personal in any of this, I'm replacing Cletus Workman as foreman of the Tell. In his stead, effective immediately, I'm appointing Mister Caden Bynum here. Mister Bynum is an experienced manager and is well versed in the methods the bank will employ to exact the optimum profitability from the business."

Chrissie was taken aback by these words. She saw its effect on Cletus as he directed his gaze to the person Manion had indicated.

Bynum was a strapping man with a shock of blond shoulder length hair under his wide brimmed hat. His long, square face was massive. Had he not been as large boned and muscular as he was, his face would have been almost too big for his body. Bynum smiled as Chrissie and Cletus looked at him. Chrissie stared at the gun on Bynum's hip. He looked more like a gunfighter than a manager. She glanced at his companions. They had the same appearance, the same imposing manner, and the guns. Something was very wrong about this.

Bremmer returned to his horse and mounted as Manion continued speaking.

"As a cost saving measure, I'm reducing the salary of the crew from fifty dollars a month to the more accepted standard of forty. Any of you who find that unsatisfactory are free to leave... now. And, Workman, since you are no longer employed here, you can leave the premises as well. Now."

The Tell riders came together. They spoke among themselves for a few seconds. Terry took a step forward, eyeing Manion. "Less wages ain't going to break us. We're staying on."

At the same time, Chrissie saw the look of consternation on Cletus's face and knew he was nearing his breaking point. She shook her head at him, silently asking him to hold back. Then she moved forward a few steps. Her eyes narrowed. "Mister Bremmer, just so you know, if I was considering returning to school, you just changed my mind." Her words were measured and emphatic. "I'm staying on here as well. And, Mister Manion, is it? Cletus is my friend, my good friend. He may not be foreman anymore, which I don't agree with, by the way, but he stays on the Tell as my guest, and I defy you, either of you, to tell me otherwise. Now, if you've concluded your business, you can all leave. Now."

Bremmer spoke back to her. "Mister Manion and I are leaving. But Mister Bynum and his men will remain to do their jobs." He tipped his hat to Chrissie. "Miss Tell." He and Manion turned their horses and rode out.

Bynum and the short, stocky man next to him dismounted and approached Chrissie. "How do, ma'am." Bynum's voice was as deep as he was broad. "This is my top hand, Pete Rawls, here."

Rawls tipped his hat but said nothing.

Chrissie flashed a frown. Her words were slow, holding back anger. "Terry is our top hand."

Bynum shook his head. "Not no more. They give me free rein

here. I say Pete's top hand." He directed his attention to Terry. "Take it or leave out."

Terry stood his ground. "Told you I'm staying."

Bynum moved in front of Cletus. He stood half a head taller than Cletus. "I ain't going to have trouble with you, am I?"

Cletus's gaze did not waver. "Not less'n it's trouble you causes."

7

A SHORT DISTANCE AWAY FROM the ranch, on the main road to Fort Worth, Bremmer and Manion rode at an unhurried pace.

"Pull up a minute." Manion reined in.

Bremmer stopped beside him.

"You said firing that nigga would get rid of him," Manion said. "Yet he's still there. I don't like this."

Bremmer voiced his displeasure. "There isn't much you do like, is there? Look, I can't foresee every eventuality. Besides, we've got to keep this at some semblance of legality. That girl is scrappier than I expected. I wouldn't put it past her to bring some kind of legal action against us if she suspects we're not above board. We can't have that."

"I still don't like it. I know you think I'm just an old wash-woman, but my fears are well founded. Workman being there is a threat. As long as he's there, even as a guest, the Tell hands will stay with him."

Bremmer gave that a moment's thought. "Then we'll make staying more difficult for him. When do you expect Bynum to report to you?"

"In a few days. Why?"

"I want you to have him set something up...."

THE FOLLOWING WEEK WAS TENSE as Bynum and his friends moved into the bunkhouse, displacing Cletus and three of the Tell riders, relegating them to makeshift quarters in the barn. As the milder weather of developing spring took hold, sleeping in the unheated barn was not the burden it would have been in the dead of winter. It was, however, uncomfortable at best.

At the north range, where the bulk of the Tell herd grazed, Bynum directed the combined group in tending the cattle and keeping strays to a minimum.

On a knoll a short distance from the activity, Cletus sat his horse, now as an observer. His job now, as he saw it, was to be a watchdog, to monitor the activities of Bynum and his friends. He did not trust the man, and he made no secret of it by his actions.

The hands conducted the routine daily operation of moving the herd to better grazing lands. From his vantage point, Cletus had a wide view of the activities. He found nothing out of the ordinary until Bynum sought Terry out. After a short conversation with Terry, Bynum led his friends away from the area. Curious, Cletus waited until the group was out of sight, then he directed his mount down the slope and rode straight to Terry.

"Where they get off to?"

Terry shrugged. "Heading back. Bynum said he got to make a report'r something. The rest said they was tired. Said we can handle this on our own."

"Tired from what? I be watching 'em. They don't do nothing. And they surely don't look nor act like wranglers, not the way they wear them guns. I'll bet they ain't here for working."

Terry nodded. "You might could be on to something there. I got a uneasy feeling about 'em as well. Good they left out though. We don't need 'em. We got this." He moved on toward the herd.

Cletus, his mind going full bore, followed. "I'll give you a hand."

As they rejoined the herd, Cletus's attention was seized by a cloud of dust rising from the west. He knew of no other herds in these parts, so it had to represent riders, a good number of them. "Hey, Terry." By the time Terry heard his call, the dust drew close enough to be identified as a group of horsemen riding hard toward them.

Terry looked toward where Cletus pointed. "Shit! They surely ain't looking friendly."

As a precaution, Cletus pulled his rifle from its saddle holster and levered a round into the chamber. Terry reached into his saddle bag and came out with a Remington revolver. They came together as the intruders could be seen plainly now. There were six of them, and each had a hand gun drawn and ready.

"Get them beeves moving," Terry shouted at the hands near the herd. "Stampede 'em."

The cowboys reacted quickly, riding at the cattle, hollering to scare the herd into fleeing.

Cletus and Terry remained in position. The raiders approached, and the lead man opened fire, followed by his companions. Cletus shouldered the rifle and fired, dropping one of the attackers. Terry joined in, but his two rounds hit nothing.

Realizing they were sitting ducks, Cletus gestured to Terry to get in front of the herd. He intended to stay between the herd and the attackers to provide some measure of protection. He saw the raiders veer off into a route that would cut the two off from the herd. Cletus and Terry pushed hard to outrun the intruders but in doing so were unable to return accurate fire.

From the far side of the herd, the Tell riders tried to lay cover fire with revolvers to distract the attackers from Cletus and Terry, but they were cowboys, not gunmen. A couple were just out of range. The rest made noise and spent lead but missed horribly. The diversion did allow Cletus and Terry some latitude in their escape attempt as the cover fire distracted the intruders. Two of the outlaws split off and rode at the herd to engage the cowboys.

Riding at full gallop, Cletus glanced back to see one of the two fall from his horse. There was no question that the man had been shot, but it was not from Terry's gun nor from his own. Then another fell in the same manner. Now the gang was down to three. Cletus pulled up short and turned his horse toward the group. He fired a rifle bullet that took another man out of the saddle.

The remaining two broke it off and rode hard in the direction they had come. It was then that Cletus heard another rifle shot in the distance. He looked that way to see a lone rider on a big gray horse perched on the knoll Cletus had occupied earlier. The man fired a final rifle shot at the fleeing outlaws. Cletus studied the rider and the horse. Shawnee and Gray.

Cletus took a fleeting look around to see Terry continuing to ride toward the herd. He heard Terry holler at the cowboys to end the stampede.

Cletus stayed in place, watching as Shawnee started down the slope. Reaching level ground, he came straight at Cletus and pulled up three feet in front of him, a broad smile on his weathered young face.

Cletus studied him. "How do you do that?"

Staring back, a confused look on his face, Shawnee replaced the rifle in its scabbard without looking. "Do what?"

"You got a knack for showing up at just the right minute. How do you do that?"

Shawnee shrugged. "Never thought about it. Just luck, I'd say."

"Well, I'm right glad to see you. Still shooting good, I see."

Shawnee grinned. "It's what keeps me alive."

Cletus nodded. "I reckon."

"Got the buffalos joined up with the beeves. Took a spell, but they getting real friendly-like. What the hell's going on here?"

Cletus looked around to see the Tell hands taking control of the cattle. "Rustlers'd be my guess. But they's a lot been going on last couple weeks, a hell of a lot."

"Fill me in."

Cletus shook his head in disgust. "Mister Tell done died and left us with a hell of a mess."

"Wait, wait, Mister Tell's dead?" Shocked, Shawnee stared off into the distance, appearing to try to comprehend the event.

"Yes, sir."

Shawnee scrunched up his face. "Well, shit...."

Cletus continued. "That ain't the all of it...."

When he'd heard it all, Shawnee shook his head in disbelief. "I was fixing to move on when I got done with the buffalos, but now I reckon not. Kind a looks like Gray and me might could lend a hand."

Cletus nodded. "Reckon you can, and welcome."

Shawnee looked toward the cattle. "Well, come on then. Let's go settle that herd down." He urged Gray forward, leaving Cletus staring at the knoll.

Jolted back to reality by Shawnee passing him, Cletus pulled his horse around and took out after Shawnee. As he rode, he regarded the man he'd only gotten a glimpse of days earlier. A little stockier after four years, not as thin, but just as fit, kind of filled out. None the worse for the obvious wear life on the run likely put him through but just as ready to chuck it all to help a friend. Still rode like the wind and shot like an expert, two skills he'd needed to stay alive this long. And that big gray horse—Gray he called him—still as feisty as ever. They made quite a pair.

Shawnee and Cletus reached the herd as the cowboys controlled the stampede. They slowed their mounts to prevent spooking the herd again. As the hands gentled the cattle, Terry split off from them and approached Shawnee and Cletus. "What the hell was that?" He pulled up close to them.

"Whatever it was, it didn't work."

"Looks like we got some help we wasn't expecting." Terry regarded Shawnee. "Thanks."

Shawnee smiled. "Sure thing."

Cletus grinned. "Say howdy to ol' Shawnee, here, Terry. He used to was you."

Shawnee and Terry shook hands.

"I don't follow."

Cletus leaned on his saddlehorn. "Shawnee worked the Tell about four years ago. He was my top hand for a good part of that. Moved on 'fore you come."

Terry smiled. "Sure had good timing. Good with that long gun, as well."

"Glad I could help." Shawnee's smile disappeared. "Appears there's a heap more going on here'n I ciphered."

"Maybe even more'n that." Cletus shook his head again. "That lawyer done fired my ass, and the banker man cut the boys' wages. Told 'em they don't like it they can mosey—"

Terry broke in. "But we staying, no matter what,"

Cletus continued. "Right, we none of us leaving Miss Chrissie high and dry."

"Yeah, about Chrissie," Shawnee said. "How's she holding up?"

"She strong, she be all right. She got her own troubles. Boss made that lawyer her guardian till she come of age. She ain't happy with that."

"Should've been you, truth be told."

"Yeah, well, my color ain't letting that happen. Boss knew that, I reckon. Y'know, I'm just wondering on something here. Them rustlers, they showed up just a short spell after that new foreman and his crew headed out. Wonder if they's some kind a connection there. We surely could a used they help, but they wasn't here."

Shawnee frowned. "I'd call him on that, I was you."

"Damn good idea. I'll do just that." Cletus pulled his horse away from the group.

Shawnee moved out behind him. "I'll side you."

Terry joined them. "Me, too."

Cletus stopped. "No, Terry, you stay right here. You in charge a this herd."

Terry nodded and pulled away.

Shawnee joined Cletus. Both went to a gallop, heading for the ranch house. During the ride, Cletus dwelled on the possible correlation between Bynum and the rustlers. He had no proof, but it just felt like it fit. The more he thought on it, the angrier he became.

Cletus was in the lead as he and Shawnee raced into the yard. He glanced at the corral to see unsaddled horses in there that belonged to Bynum and his friends. Cletus reined in hard and was out of the saddle before his horse stopped. Shawnee dismounted as Cletus moved purposefully toward the bunkhouse, stopping ten feet from the entrance. Shawnee fell in a few feet behind Cletus, off to the side. As mad as he was, Cletus had the presence of mind to know his friend was there, backing him up.

"Bynum!" Cletus's voice boomed, leaving no doubt it would be heard. He waited, staring at the door.

In a few seconds, the door opened, and Bynum stepped out, an annoyed expression on his face. "What the hell you doing here?" He glance Shawnee's way. "Who the hell is that?

Cletus growled out. "He's a friend."

"Hell do you want, anyhow?"

"I want answers." Cletus's determination was apparent.

Bynum glared. "You ain't asked nothing yet."

"The north range herd just got hit by rustlers. Thanks to Shawnee here, we drove 'em off, dropped a few as well. You and your boys being there would a helped, but you done rode out... just 'fore they come. I want to know why."

Bynum's scowl was ominous. "Now, you wait a minute, boy."

As he spoke, his three companions appeared behind him. They spread out on both sides of him.

Cletus fumed and clenched his teeth. "My name is Cletus Workman. You don't call me 'boy.'"

Bynum moved slowly toward him. "I'll call you anything I want. And you don't accuse me of something just 'cause you reckon so. Why, I ought to whomp you good." Bynum kept coming, faster now. "Damn nigga!" He swung a wide, slow left fist at Cletus. Ready for it, welcoming it, Cletus ducked under the blow. His left came up from below his knees into Bynum's solar plexus, doubling the man over and sapping his wind. He grunted as the fist pushed into him. Cletus straightened up and aimed a right in a chop. The heal of his fist hit Bynum's left ear, slamming him in a wide arc and dumping him heavily on the ground on his side. Blood oozed from his ear as Cletus recovered his stance.

Behind him, Cletus heard Shawnee's voice. "No way you'll make it, friend." Cletus glanced to that side. Shawnee stood with his side arm drawn and trained on Pete Rawls. Rawls froze in mid-draw.

"Drop it. Two fingers."

Rawls complied, lifting the gun out of its holster with thumb and forefinger. He let it fall.

Bynum, holding his wounded ear, rose with some effort, grimacing in pain.

Cletus took a step closer. "Now, you listen to me, you son of a bitch. You get your shit together, and you get off the Tell. We don't need your kind here. Come back here again, and it won't be fists you're facing. Now git!"

Seething, Bynum appeared to think better of a second attempt at fighting Cletus. He turned slowly and staggered back into the bunkhouse. Rawls tried to bend down to retrieve his revolver.

"Leave it." Shawnee's voice was low and threatening.

Rawls straightened up and went back inside, followed by the other two. Shawnee moved to where Rawls's gun lay and picked it up. Holstering his own piece, he quickly flipped the caps off the revolver's nipples, rendering it unprepared to fire.

Unwavering, Cletus stood by.

Within a few minutes, the four men emerged carrying their belongings. Bynum still nursed his wound, cupping his hand over the ear. Blood ran down the hand and onto the sleeve of his shirt.

Cletus met them as they stepped through the doorway. "Saddle up and git."

As Rawls moved forward, Shawnee took a step closer and inserted Rawls's pistol in his holster. Shawnee said nothing, but the look he shot at Rawls told the man he'd best move on quietly.

They filed into the corral and went through the motions of saddling their horses.

As they mounted, Bynum glared at Cletus. "You ain't heard the last a me. I'll see you in hell."

"Anytime you feel lucky, I'm here."

Shawnee broke in. "Enough talk. Get to riding."

Bynum glared. "You'll be sorry you mixed into this."

Shawnee met his gaze. "Look to yourself, friend. I ain't the sorry one." He lifted out his revolver and pointed it at them. "Last call. Move out."

Bynum led his three companions out of the corral and toward the main trail leading to Fort Worth. Shawnee and Cletus watched them leave.

"You ain't changed much," Shawnee said. "Those fists still work real good."

Cletus shrugged. "That weren't much. Seen that swing coming 'fore he even thunk it up. But look here. What we just done? Ain't no coming back from that. We in it for good and all now. And they'll be back, guaranteed. You sure you want a piece of this?"

Shawnee holstered his gun. "Yeah, Cletus, I'm sure."

Behind them, a female voice called out. "Shawnee."

8

SHAWNEE KNEW THAT VOICE. HE turned toward it and smiled. "How do, Chrissie?"

Chrissie Tell stood on the big ranch house porch, her mouth open in surprise.

Paying no heed to her awkwardness, Shawnee looked at her fondly, taking in the beauty four years had only added to her face and figure. This was the girl, now a woman, he considered his first love. The very same girl he had avoided during the time he worked at the Tell because his past would have dragged her into a life of running from the law. None of that had changed. A union of the two could never be, he knew that, but he still held that spot in his heart for her. Navigating his commitment to helping the Tell would be tricky if Chrissie still felt the same about him. This might take some careful stepping.

He removed his hat and stood there. She moved toward him, slowly at first, then hurried, stopping two feet from him.

"What... what are you doing here?" Her voice conveyed disbelief. "I thought you... Cletus said you—"

"I run into your pa on his way back from Dakota. Been seeing to the buffalo calves. I can't tell you how sorry I be about your pa. He done took me in and give me a chance, and I owe him for that. I'm here to help. My way of paying that debt."

Chrissie regained some of her composure. "Thank you, Shawnee. It's good to see you again. You're welcome to stay for as long as you want."

Those words seemed a tad distant and formal to Shawnee, but he knew Chrissie had a reason for it. Maybe she held back because Cletus stood nearby. Or maybe she realized this couldn't get personal between them. Or maybe she didn't feel the same about him. Whatever her motive, she made things easier for him. "Thank you kindly, Chrissie. I surely wish things was different."

Chrissie's face showed the sorrow in her heart. "I know. We all do, but we can't change what's already done."

"True enough. But we can surely see it don't get no worse."

Chrissie smiled as she moved closer to him. "Pa thought an awful lot of you. Would you like to go to his grave to pay your respects?"

Shawnee nodded. "Yeah, I'd admire to do that."

"We can go now if you like. I'll show you where it is."

"I reckon we can go now." He was a tad unsure of her intentions.

"All right, I'll get my horse." She left them and entered the barn.

Cletus mounted. "I'm heading back out. See you later."

Shawnee nodded, preoccupied, looking back toward Chrissie. "Yeah... later."

SHAWNEE ACCOMPANIED CHRISSIE ON THE ride to Bruno Tell's gravesite. It was slow, allowing them to speak unencumbered. Chrissie voiced her curiosity.

"Shawnee, why did you leave? Cletus said you got in some kind of trouble up in Kansas, and you just up and left the drive, but he never said what that trouble was."

"Reckon I done some things, Chrissie, things that needed doing, only the law didn't see it that way. There wasn't no way I was bringing that back on the Tell, on you folks, not after what your pa did for me, giving me a chance, learning me, and all. So, I went to running right then, and truth be told, I been on the run ever since."

"I can't believe you're guilty of anything, not the Shawnee I knew. Isn't there something you can do to clear yourself?"

Shawnee took a long breath. "Lot of things got done back then. Some was my fault, some not. Reckon I'm too far into it now to get clear of it. I just got to stay as many jumps ahead of the law as I can and try to help as many folks as I can along the way. Kind a like what I'm doing here."

"I don't care what the law says you did. I know who you are, and you're not a criminal."

"I got to tell you, Chrissie, there's damn few'd agree with you on that point."

They stopped and dismounted at the two cottonwoods that stood guard over the graves of Selena and Bruno Tell. Dropping their reins, they walked to Chrissie's father's grave.

Shawnee noted the age span between Tell's birth and death dates. Fifty-eight years. Not young but for someone of Tell's spirit, not an age for dying. "Surely is a shame," he said aloud. He heard a sniffle from Chrissie and turned to see a tear running down her cheek. She was staring at the grave marker. Feeling he was the cause of her tears, he berated himself. "Chrissie, I'm sorry. I shouldn't ought a made you come out here."

Chrissie sucked in a breath. "It's all right." Her voice quivered. "It was my choice. I've got to learn to deal with this."

"I should a knowed, should a thought...."

She turned to face him and pulled in another deep breath. Her hand went to his forearm. "Shawnee, I'm glad you came back. I really missed you."

Shawnee smiled. He couldn't hold back acknowledging his feelings. "Yeah, well, that said, I missed you as well."

And then her arms wrapped around him, and she awkwardly laid her head on his shoulder. She whimpered and held on to him tightly.

"Chrissie...."

She murmured. "Hold me."

"Chrissie—"

"Please."

Instinctively, but against his better judgment, he put his arms around her and held her. She melted into him and cried openly. He was touched by her need for him, realizing he should have known this would happen. Now committed, he had to see it through.

Chrissie stayed in the safe place of Shawnee's embrace for a few minutes as she tried to regain herself. She lifted her head and leaned back, her face close to his. She hesitated, then reached up and kissed him softly. He felt the tears on her cheeks rub off on his own. Unable to contain himself, he kissed her back for a second, then realized he'd let this go too far. He pulled his head back.

She stared into his eyes. He saw the pain there, the loss, the same feeling he'd known when he lost his own parents. This had to be just comforting her, he told himself, nothing more.

"I... I'm sorry." She spoke softly, with almost no voice. "I shouldn't have.... It's just so hard."

"I know how it is. But you got to be strong."

She nodded. "I know, but it's... I feel so... alone."

Those words brought home to Shawnee the exact same feelings

he experienced every day alone on the trail. But she was different, her situation was different. "Chrissie, you ain't never going to be alone. You got Cookie and the Tell wranglers, and you got Cletus. He'll never leave you, you know that."

"I know, but it's not the same."

"Ain't nobody can replace your pa, not Cletus, not me, I know that. And I'll be here to help long as I'm needed, but that's got to be the all of it. It's you got to hold onto the Tell—you, for your pa."

Chrissie studied Shawnee. Maybe she was drawing strength from him or something like that. She drew in a cleansing breath and cleared her throat. "You're right." Her voice was stronger now. She braced herself and stood a little taller. "There's work to be done."

Shawnee smiled. "There you go. That's the Chrissie I know."

———

ALONE IN HIS OFFICE, MANION responded to a knock on the back door. As he opened it, his face showed surprise at Bynum standing there, hat in hand, a bandage around his head covering his ear. Blood drippings were prominent on his shirt. "What the hell happened to you?"

Bynum stepped inside. "Just come from the doc's. Had a run-in with that nigga. Slugged me when I wasn't looking."

Manion closed the door. "What did you do to tick him off?"

"Nothing. He's already ticked off 'cause he's out." Bynum went to Manion's desk and sat in the guest chair.

Manion stepped in front of Bynum. "Did your... um, *friends...* get the cattle?"

"Naw, they got drove off. Some stranger mixed in, dropped a few of 'em. Some kind of gunsel, I reckon, the way they said he was shooting." Bynum saw a look of concern cross Manion's face as he moved to his desk and sat down.

"That's not good. We were counting on the loss of the cattle to weaken the Tell."

"That ain't the half of it. The nigga and that stranger come back to the bunkhouse after they chased my boys away. He said I was part of it. Course I denied it, but they run us off the Tell anyhow. Said there'd be worse waiting for us, we come back."

Manion was instantly unnerved. "Damn it, Bynum, you came with high recommendations. My contacts said you could handle yourself no—"

"Stranger pulled iron on us. We had no chance."

Manion thought for a moment. "All right, we can still salvage this. We just need to get rid of Workman."

Bynum smiled. "I'll handle that. I owe him. He'll never know what hit him."

"No, that's not what I meant. If you kill him, the law will start asking questions we don't want asked."

Bynum was puzzled. "Well, how do you want it done?"

Manion pondered again. "We can still put Workman in a bind. It'll take some lying on your part, but what I've got in mind should work. Go talk to the state police sergeant, Malahide. Tell him about your run-in with Workman. He interfered with you doing your job. When you called him on it, he knocked you down and chased you off at gunpoint. Say he threatened you. While you're there, tell him you've been watching Workman, and you suspect he set up the rustling. If he questions you further about it, make up something, but keep it simple."

Bynum was instantly turned off. "Now, wait a damn minute here. I don't want to be talking to no lawman."

"You have nothing to worry about. Look, you're a concerned citizen who was trying to do the job you were hired to do. Workman is preventing you from doing that, and he could be guilty of worse."

Bynum shook his head. "I still don't like it."

"Frankly, I don't like the idea of getting the law involved, but in this case, it can help us. And you're not getting paid to like it. You're getting paid to do whatever you're told. There's too much tied up in this to back out now."

Bynum tried to put off contact with the law. "I don't know. Maybe we ought to run this by Bremmer."

Manion became defensive. "There's no need for that. I'm perfectly capable of handling this. Besides, Bremmer's out of town. If we can get Malahide to lean on Workman, that nigga'll think twice about interfering again. Now, do as I tell you. Go see Malahide and say what I told you."

Bynum still tried to delay. "Now?"

"Yes, now."

Bynum, realizing he was out of options, got up and left the office. He walked the two blocks to the building housing the location of the State Police in the front and the jail in the rear. Not an enthusiast of lawmen, or the law in general, he entered hesitantly.

At a table facing Bynum, Texas State Police Sergeant Earl Malahide sat writing. Papers scattered around the surface gave the impression that the officer was disorganized. Bynum noted, however, that there seemed to be an order to the clutter as Malahide selected individual pages for reference as he wrote in his journal.

Bynum's interest did not linger on Malahide's methods. He wanted only to make the report and get out of the lawman's presence. He approached the table.

Malahide was stocky, even pudgy, but solid enough to hold his own in a fight. His face was round, with dark eyes and a constant scowl. Almost bald, he wore a full handlebar mustache and a scruff beard. He was dressed in a dark, wrinkled suit with a collarless white shirt. The badge pinned to his lapel was in the shape of a shield, engraved with lettering that spelled out *Texas State Police Sergeant.*

He looked up. "Help you?" His voice was deep, with a wide Southern accent.

"I want to... eh... well, report something." Bynum couldn't hide his uneasiness.

"I can help you with that." Malahide set aside his journal and cleared an opening in the papers. Then he pulled a clean sheet to the center and prepared to write. "What's your name?"

"Cade Bynum."

Malahide wrote the name down. "And what'd you want to report?"

Bynum sucked in a breath, intending to get this out without hesitation. "Well, I just got hired on as the foreman of the Tell Ranch a couple weeks back. The bank fired the *hombre* that used to was the foreman, so I'm there to replace him. Problem is, he's still hanging around there, and he's making it hard for me doing my job." Bynum squirmed a little. He hoped Malahide didn't notice. Malahide's expression didn't change, so he couldn't tell if he did. "Keeps telling me how to do things, and I'm doing stuff wrong. I finally called him on it. He turns around and slugs me when I ain't looking." He pointed to the bandage. "Then he pulls a gun on me and runs me off the place. Told me I come back, he'll plug me."

Malahide was quiet while he recorded Bynum's statement. "What name's this fellow go by?"

"Cletus Workman." Bynum said the name very plainly.

"Black man, ain't he?"

"Yeah, what's that got to do with it?"

"Just making sure him being black ain't what's driving this, friend. Can't do that no more, y'know, not after a war was fought and lost over it."

"Naw, that ain't it." Bynum now dug in, acting as if what he was saying was true. "Look, I got nothing agin him. I'm just trying to make good on this job, and he keeps getting in my way. I don't know what's eating him. Maybe 'cause I got the job he got let off of, but that ain't my fault. I just want him to back off is all."

Malahide looked up from his paper. "You looking to file charges agin him?"

Bynum raised his hand in a negative gesture. "No, nothing like that. I don't know, maybe you just palaver with him, set him straight, you being the law and all."

Malahide put down his pencil. "I reckon I can do that. Maybe he don't savvy what could come of this. He still at the Tell?"

"He made it powerful clear he ain't leaving, so I reckon he is."

"All right, I'll take a ride out to there and read him chapter and verse. That ought to settle him down."

Bynum nodded. "Yeah, yeah, that ought to do it."

Malahide got up and reached behind him for his hat. "Likely better I handle this alone. Don't want you two tangling again. You stay in town till I get 'er done."

Bynum nodded again. "Yeah, sure, whatever you say."

Malahide started for the door, but Bynum didn't move. "There something else?"

Bynum stared at the wall. "Well, maybe...." He hesitated, trying to form the words.

"Come on, man, spit it out."

Bynum forced himself to continue. "We had some rustlers hit one a the herds, but they got drove off. Just fore that happened,

Workman got real scarce for a spell. I can't shake the feeling he maybe had something to do with that rustling."

"You prove that?" Malahide showed interest.

Bynum shook his head. "Naw, just a notion I got. Mighty funny him disappearing just fore it happened. The rustling, I mean."

Malahide was quiet for a few seconds. "I'll take it from here."

IT WAS EVENING. THE LONE rider on the road leading from Fort Worth to the Tell was just a shadow against the rising moon. Shawnee and Cletus led the last of the Tell horses from the corral toward the barn where they would be bedded down for the night.

Shawnee spotted the approaching visitor. "Rider coming."

Cletus looked in the direction of the main road where the figure could be seen. "Can't make him out." They waited, halting the horses.

The rider continued at the same slow pace. Within minutes, he arrived in the yard and drew rein, leaning forward and adjusting himself in the saddle. "Evening, gents."

Shawnee and Cletus both replied with a greeting. Neither indicated recognition of the caller.

"I reckon you'd be Cletus Workman."

"That's right."

"Sergeant Malahide with the State Police. I got a complaint about you." Malahide lifted his lapel to display his badge.

"That so?"

Shawnee remained silent and watched as Cletus played this cagey, saying only the bare minimum.

"Yup. You know an *hombre* name a Cade Bynum?"

"We met."

"Did more'n meet to hear him tell it. Says you clocked him and run him off hereabouts. Also says you pulled a gun on him, threatened to shoot him. What you got to say about that?"

"He took a swing at me. I swung back. He went down."

"What about the gun?"

"I never pulled no gun."

Malahide looked Cletus over. "You be wearing one."

"Wearing and pulling's two different things."

Shawnee took a step forward. "I can vouch for that. I's standing right there. No gun."

Malahide shot a glance at Shawnee. "And who might you be?"

"They call me Shawnee."

"That the whole of it?"

Shawnee nodded. "All I need."

Malahide's eyes narrowed. "Man don't use his given name, I get a tad suspicious. What's your stake in this?"

"Friend of the Tells is all."

Malahide studied Shawnee for a moment. "I get the feeling I seen you before. Kind a look familiar-like."

"Not likely. Ain't been in these parts for years."

Malahide scrunched his face. "I got a real good memory. It'll come to me if it's there. You sure there wasn't no gun?"

"Look, Cletus told you how it happened. I'm saying he ain't lying. That's how it was. No gun."

"So you say." Malahide turned his attention back to Cletus. "I'm curious. Bynum said you ain't foreman here no more, that he is. How come you're still here and look to be working when you ain't getting paid?"

"Like Shawnee said, I's a friend of the Tells. Just looking out for Miss Chrissie."

Malahide shot Cletus an uncertain look. "Bynum also says there was a rustling try. Says you went off for a spell just before. Thinks there might be a connection twixt the two."

Shawnee watched Cletus tense up, bunch up his fists, then take a breath and relax.

Cletus breathed again. "Just the rustling happened is all. I never went off."

"You prove that?"

Cletus didn't hesitate. "The hands'll back me on it, but I don't see where I gots to prove nothing to nobody."

Malahide took a moment as he appeared to digest everything. "Tell you what. I'm letting that go for now, but I'm warning you, and this is official, Bynum's foreman here. You tangle with him again, I'm coming back here with a warrant... for you. You savvy?"

Cletus tensed again. "Yeah."

Malahide turned his horse to leave. "See you abide by it."

9

"WHY?" BREMMER'S VOICE RESOUNDED IN Manion's office as he reacted to learning the events that occurred during his absence. He and Bynum were seated in the guest chairs facing Manion's desk. Bremmer leaned forward, glaring at Manion.

Manion replied matter-of-factly. "Workman needed to be taken down a peg. He's got to understand he's not in charge anymore. And it was a chance to throw the rustling scheme on him."

"No! We handle it ourselves." Bremmer's voice was still raised. "We don't get the law involved."

"We've got the law on our side."

Bremmer, now fuming, rose and paced half the length of the room. "If you were trying to sabotage this operation, you couldn't have done a better job." He turned to face Manion. "We might have the law on our side, but we don't need its participation. Have you forgotten that what we're doing here is not exactly legal?" He directed the tirade at Bynum. "And you, are you telling me, as big as you are, you couldn't take that black man down?"

Bynum turned sharply in his chair. "I done told you, he hit me when I wasn't looking."

"I don't care." Bremmer took a step closer to Bynum. "You should have been looking, all the time. Now we've got that lawman nosing around. What did he tell you after he talked to Workman?"

"He said he warned him if he tangles with me again, he'd arrest him. He left it at that."

"And the rustling?"

Bynum shook his head. "Didn't say nothing about that."

"And, of course, you didn't ask."

Bynum shot back. "Hey, I didn't want no part a no lawman first off. Ain't never had no good dealings with 'em. Got shed a him quick as I could."

Bremmer stopped to think, huffing a breath. "All right, that's as far as this goes. For the time being, you stay away from the Tell. Stay in town." He paced again for a few seconds, continuing to think. "Our best bet for the present is to find a way to force Workman and those cowboys off the Tell."

Bynum piped up. "Me and my boys can put 'em all down."

"No!" Bremmer shouted, glaring at Bynum. "God damn it! What part of having no lawmen involved do you not understand? That's all we'd need is for Workman and his friends to turn up dead. That state policeman would really start digging then." He thought again for a moment. "No, it's got to be something that cripples the operation and cuts off their wages at the same time. If the ranch, say, is losing money, we can stop their pay without drawing suspicion on us. Then they'll have to leave on their own."

Manion broke in. "But Workman is already staying without pay. That didn't seem to change his mind."

"I doubt the others will be so loyal. Once they're gone, even if the nigga stays, how much damage can one man do? Now, think. What will bring everything to a halt?"

All three pondered. Several minutes passed.

Bynum looked up. "Well, they can't work cattle without horses."

Bremmer returned to his seat. "All right, that's a start. What have you got in mind?"

"Round up all their horses and hide 'em out somewheres."

Bremmer nodded slowly. "Good. That'll give us good reason to let them all go."

Manion added a thought. "Adjustments could be made to the books to make it look like the ranch has been losing money."

Bremmer nodded excessively. "Of course, that'll do it."

Then he looked back at Bynum. "How long will it take for you get your part done?"

"A day, maybe two. Got to find a good place to hide the horses. Soon as we got that, we can go grab 'em,"

"In the meantime, send one of your men to watch the Tell. We need to know their every move, the best time to move on the horses. Get to it."

Bynum rose and left the office.

Bremmer glared at Manion. "Now, you hear me, Manion." He spoke through his teeth. "Your idea about the books does not cancel your previous blunder. From here on, nobody makes decisions about this but me. Do you understand?"

Manion lowered his eyes to focus on the desk. "Shit! I just wish this was over with."

"Do you understand?"

"Yes."

CHRISSIE STRODE ACROSS THE YARD toward the bunkhouse on a night bright with the light of a full moon. There was purpose in her as she walked quickly, having made a decision she had pondered for several days. She stopped at the bunkhouse door and knocked, aware that barging in might expose her to men in varying stages of dress, or in this case, undress.

The door opened, revealing top hand Terry, almost fully clothed. "Evening, Miss Chrissie."

"Good evening, Terry. I, uh... I'd like to talk to everyone. I hope I'm not intruding."

Terry smiled and looked over his shoulder. "Hey, get yourself decent in there. We got a lady visitor."

A scurry of movements came from inside. It lasted for a few seconds. Terry glanced again over his shoulder and turned back to Chrissie. "I reckon they're decent as they'll ever get." He stepped aside.

Chrissie went in and took a position in the center of the long, one-room building. Cletus sat on an end bunk taking haphazard white thread stitches to close a tear in a red shirt. Shawnee sat on the floor next to him, cleaning his side arm. The others were spotted at bunks throughout the place.

Chrissie took a breath. "I have something I need to say. I've been thinking about this since my father passed. Most of you came to the Tell years ago in search of not only a job but a place away from the war, maybe even away from the law. My father took you in, no questions asked. The Tell became your safe place because he made it that way. The only thing he asked of you in return was loyalty, loyalty to him and to the Tell. You gave that willingly." This elicited nods and low murmurs of agreement from the men.

Chrissie smiled. "Now he's gone, and the Tell is struggling to survive. But still, you stand by it, even though you're losing money on the deal. I know my father would appreciate that, and I know you appreciated him and what he did for you. I know that's why you're staying on. So, I'd like us to take a day, this coming Sunday I thought, for a memorial to him and to the Tell. We'll have a cook-out. We can celebrate him and his life and his work to make the Tell the biggest and best spread in Texas. Anyone who has anything they'd like to say about him or the Tell or anything else really will be welcome to speak. What do you think of that?"

Several answers sounded at the same time, all in agreement. Then a few men made statements to the effect that working at the Tell saved their necks or gave them a home when no one else would.

Cletus nodded. "Mister Tell give me my freedom. I'd likely be dead without him."

Shawnee looked up. "Same here. He gave me a chance when I needed it most. Truth be told, the Tell's the closest thing to a home I had since I left Kansas. Wisht I could stay on, but that's my doing."

Shawnee's admission hit Chrissie hard. She forced a grin. "All right, then. It's settled. I'll talk to Cookie and get it set up. I know Pa would appreciate it. Besides, I think we all need a little break from things past and things coming." Caught up in her emotions, she turned abruptly for the door, biting her lip to hold back a tear. She'd hoped against hope he'd change his mind and stay, but now it was clear to her. Her heart broke again as she accepted that there'd be no future life with Shawnee. Halfway to the house, the tears came full on.

DAWN ON THE RANGE ROUSED Pete Rawls from a slumber under the stars. He had been sent by Bynum to watch the Tell and report back any possibilities that arose to facilitate the theft of the ranch's

horses. His camp was tucked into a thick underbrush about a mile
east of the Tell ranch house, off the main road by just a few yards. It
was a cold camp to avoid detection while hiding so close. No fire, no
cooking. He ate jerky and pemmican and drank water from a nearby
stream. He slept bundled in a warm coat and two heavy wool blankets. This was an unpleasant assignment to say the least. Why him?
He was supposed to be Bynum's top hand, his number two. One of
the other guys could have done this just as easy. Still, the money was
good, so he'd endure it and hope it would be short lived.

This was the third day of his vigil, Sunday he was pretty sure. As
he rolled out of his coverings, he noticed it was warmer this morning
than the previous two. The air was still and quiet, and there was a
promise of clear skies and a mild breeze, not the usual gusty winds of
the plains. He stood up and stretched, grunting. The ground was hard,
not very comfortable for sleeping, and caused some aches and pains.

Before anything, he needed a look at the Tell and its operations.
His saddle bag was lashed to the saddle that lay on the ground acting
as his pillow. He reached in and pulled out a spyglass. Putting it to
his eye, he adjusted the lens and scanned the area.

The routine hadn't changed in the past two days. The only thing
out of the ordinary was the way the girl and that stranger, the one
who'd throwed down on him, watched each other without the other one knowing. Likely something between them, maybe sweet on
each other or the like. He'd shrugged that off as unimportant.

Ranch hands typically rose at dawn and prepared for a long day's
work, no matter what the day of the week. He'd worked enough
of these wrangler jobs to know running cattle was a daily grind. It
never considered weekends as anything other than another day of
work. Some waddies got off for a day somewhere during the week,
but that was on a rotating basis. Rawls recollected that. His stays at

ranches all over were always the same. The nature of the business was get 'er done, every day, no matter what. He counted that as the chief reason ranch work was not for him.

He watched for a good half hour. What he saw this day was strange. There was no saddling up this day. Truth be told, there was very little activity at all. The Tell hands piled out of the bunkhouse and into the cook shack, likely for breakfast, no matter how late it was, but then nothing further happened. They just went back to the bunkhouse and hung out. Curious. He continued to observe.

Another fifteen minutes passed. Two men emerged from the bunkhouse, saddled up, and rode out to the north. No one else left. Rawls's curiosity increased, as did his appetite. He broke out his meager food and munched as he surveyed for further activity.

It took an hour before anything more occurred. At that time, the girl left the main house, crossed the yard, and entered the bunk-house. Within minutes, she and the men spilled out into the yard. Several of the men, the black man among them, carried a long table from the cook shack into the yard. Others brought chairs out and set them around the table. No attempt was made to fetch horses from the barn. It was clear nobody was going anywhere save for the yard.

What the hell were they doing? Rawls pushed his hat back on his head and scratched at his dirty hair, an indication of his confusion. He looked more intently through the lens.

A few moments later, the cook brought a large wood crate to the table, and from it he doled out dishes and utensils. He returned after a few minutes with a steaming pot, which he placed in the center of the table.

If that wasn't the start of a shindig, Rawls was at a loss for what else it might be. That could be exactly what he was waiting for. He put away the spyglass and the food and rolled his blankets. Within five minutes, he was packed up and had saddled his horse. After a final gaze through the glass that told him whatever this was would continue, he mounted and directed the animal through the bushes and onto the main road. Then he slapped the reins across the horse's hindquarters, urging an instant gallop. Bynum had set up a campsite nearby. Rawls made directly for it.

THE TELL COOKOUT PROCEEDED THROUGH breakfast. As the table was cleared, a couple of the hands brought their musical instruments, a fiddle and a banjo, from the bunkhouse and began playing random melodies. This transformed into a rendition by the two cowboys of the ballad known as "The Cowboy's Lament," the completion of which set the mood for individually offered eulogies dedicated to Bruno Tell.

Cletus rose first. "Reckon I'll start. Mister Tell and me, we go back about ten year. I's a slave back then. Worked on a plantation outside N'Orlens. My master got me trained to prize fight. Done made him a lot a money till one day I hit the man I's fighting wrong, and he died. Master took a lot a grief for that, so he decided to sell me off. I got rode into N'Orlens to the auctions. I's last to go on the block. That auctioneer, he a mean cuss. Took a disliking to me right off. Started pushing and shoving at me till I done got my fill a that, and I pushed back.

"Well, I pushed at him hard enough, he falls off a that block. He hollers at his friends to grab hold a me, and he goes and gets his whip. He's going to whup me something fierce. So, he hauls back with that there whip, and he's about to sling it at me when they's a shot. I turns to look, and I sees Mister Tell. 'Course, I didn't know him from Adam back then, but he's standing there holding his pistol on that auctioneer, and he says, 'You stop that. You got no call whupping that boy.' That auctioneer, he damn near done it in his britches right there he's so scared."

Laughter rose from the group at those words.

"Mister Tell, he pulls out a sack of coins and heaves it at that man, and he says, 'That's for the black man. He coming with me.' So me and him, we back out of there and get on some horses and ride like the wind out of there. When we gone from there, and my head stopped spinning, I weren't sure I could trust him. I asked him how come he saved me. All he said was he liked how I handled myself, and it weren't right what they was doing. Then he told me I'm a free man, and he give me a paper saying so, and he offered me a job. A job paying cash money. Me, a black man, working a job paying cash money. I couldn't hardly believe it, but it be true. I knew right then and there I could trust him. I been here with him ever since. Hadn't been for Mister Tell, I'd a likely died that day. I ain't never been able to thank him proper for that."

Shawnee remained seated as he spoke next. "Some of you waddies come here after I left, but Cletus and Cookie and Miss Chrissie, they know me. No call to rehash what brought me here, but I learned a hell of a lot from Mister Tell and from Cletus and the rest of the crew, not just about working cattle but about living your life. I'll always be grateful for that. Mister Tell was a fine man, the best, and I'll never forget him."

Shawnee glanced at Chrissie as he finished and saw tears in her eyes. She smiled at him, and he smiled back and nodded.

As the day wore on, others spoke out about their experiences with Tell and their gratitude for him being there when they needed a helping hand. The stories were diverse but similar in that each man, running from something, found a safe place to light thanks to Bruno Tell.

10

AS DUSK CREPT IN, CLEANUP began. Dishes and utensils were removed from the table and brought into the cook shack. There Cookie led the few hands who could fit in the small structure in the washing, drying, and securing of the items, while others carried the table back to its spot in the dining area. The chores were finished by nightfall.

Chrissie thanked the men for participating. "I know Pa appreciated your feelings for him. I'm glad we did this. It made me feel better, and I hope it did the same for you."

A rousing consent rose from the men.

Chrissie bid them good night and turned for the main house.

Cletus headed for the bunkhouse. "Back to work come morning. Time to turn in."

They agreed, vacating the yard and filing into the bunkhouse.

QUIET BLANKETED THE TELL AS the low light of a crescent moon joined with a cloud-filled sky to mask the few stars that might have been visible. On foot, two men bent low to keep from being seen as they moved in the fields behind the main house. Continuing to the far side of the flat tall grass plain, one man watched while the other crouched, struck a match on his pant leg, and dropped it into the dry growth. An immediate flare-up resulted. The two men hurried to the near side and performed the same act. As they scurried away, flames leapt up to begin consuming the fuel.

The fire grew, lighting the meadow with an orange and yellow glow. Running the last eighth of a mile, the men joined Rawls and two other men waiting in a thicket.

Rawls gazed at the fire. "We'll give it a few minutes to really catch. When they're all tied up with fighting it, we'll move in. Take your ropes to keep the nags together. I'll bring our mounts. Got it?"

The men nodded, then moved farther into the brush where their horses were tied. They grabbed the lariats from their saddles and stood by. Rawls continued to watch the fire spread.

TIRED FROM A FULL DAY, Chrissie slept soundly for the first time since her father's passing. The smell of smoke wafted in through the partially open window in the darkened room. It drifted across the room and settled in the air over the bed. As more accumulated, a cloud formed, and the odor reached Chrissie's nose, causing an instant disturbance. A single cough made her stir. Another caused her to awaken. As her eyes opened, the stuff became thick enough to shorten her breath and to generate further coughing. Abruptly, she was fully awake and alert.

Throwing back the covers caused the smoke to drift away, allowing her breath to return. She bounded out of bed and across to the window. As she slammed the sash closed, the glow in the distance caught her gaze. She rubbed sleep from her eyes and looked again. Fire. Raging. *Oh, God.* Pinpointing the location in the field behind the house, she padded to the bed, pulled on her robe, and hurried out of the room. She took the stairs quickly and rushed out the front door. "Cletus!" She shouted at the top of her voice as she raced across the yard in bare feet, paying no heed to dirt, stones, and other impediments. "Cletus! Shawnee!"

As she closed on the bunkhouse, the door swung open, and Cletus appeared, hitching pants on.

"Cletus, fire." Her call was accompanied by her waving gesture at the location of the blaze.

He looked in that direction. His look of surprise turned to deep concern, then panic. Over his shoulder he called into the bunkhouse. "Roll out in there. Brush fire. Come on." He ducked back inside and came back out seconds later with a blanket. As he ran toward Chrissie, who had stopped in the yard, others spilled out of the bunkhouse, Shawnee with them. They had blankets, and they ran directly at the fire, some without boots on.

Cletus stopped in front of Chrissie. "We got this. You be safest in the bunkhouse."

"No, I can help. I want to help."

Cletus raised a halting hand. "Chrissie, no. I ain't risking you getting burned. You got to stay clear a this."

"Cletus—"

"I say no." The stern look on his face backed Chrissie up a step. "Now you get yourself inside. Please, girl. I gots to keep you safe."

Chrissie took a breath, taken aback by his manner. She relented, understanding his concern and the responsibility he felt toward her. "All right. Yes, all right." She nodded, moved past him, and made for the bunkhouse.

Cletus took a moment, then went to a dead run in the direction of the field.

———————————

RAWLS WATCHED THE TELL HANDS spread out as they attacked the blaze. He signaled to his men. "Head for the barn." The four men responded to the order as Rawls went to where the horses were secured to bushes. Releasing and gathering the reins, he led the animals out to follow the men to the barn.

At the barn back door, one man attempted entry. It didn't budge. "Break it in." Rawls stopped the horses a few yards away.

Next, two men put their shoulders to the door and heaved. The door cracked as wood split under their weight. A second attempt pushed it open.

Rawls issued his next order, pointing at the two who'd crashed the door in. "You two get the nags out." He signaled the others. "Mount up and wrangle 'em." They made for their mounts. In seconds, the two men in the barn had a couple of lamps going and began bringing horses out. The two on horseback took control of the confused animals as ropes were removed from their necks. Rawls moved into nearby bushes and broke a large branch away. He stood by waiting as the operation continued.

The two thieves reentered the barn and approached Gray's stall. Immediately aware of imminent danger, the horse backed into the little cell until his hindquarters met the wall. The stall gate swung open. Gray went up on his hind legs, ready to defend incursion. The pair backed up as Gray let out a growl of protest. One man threw his lariat, the loop settling over the mount's head. The man hauled back, digging his boot heels into the earth floor, trying to pull Gray back down on his front legs. His partner threw his loop and pulled on the animal from the other side. Gray continued to struggle, straining against their strength.

"Hey, Pete, we need help with this one."

Rawls responded, carrying a rope. He positioned himself between the other two and shook out a loop. Gray continued to fight.

One man shouted at Rawls. "Let's just leave this one."

"No, Cade wants all of 'em. This one goes." His throw put a third tow on Gray. With three pulling in different directions, the horse quickly became exhausted to the point of being yanked out of the stall and into the area behind the barn. Under constant pulling and tugging, Gray was placed with the other horses.

INTENSELY CONCENTRATING ON TRYING TO control and extinguish the fire, Shawnee stood shoulder to shoulder with Cletus, swinging blankets to beat out the flames. Choking on thick smoke, Shawnee stepped back and turned away to clear his lungs with fresher air. His glance fell to the back of the house, and the angle of the blaze made something click in his brain. He leaned in to Cletus. "Damn thing's headed right for the house."

Cletus looked around. True enough. He glanced to the men on his right. "Riley! Plácido! Wet down the back a the house and the yard behind it. Go."

The two men turned in unison and raced back toward the barn.

Cletus turned to Shawnee. "Help me try to turn this thing." He and Shawnee angled themselves to try to turn the fire away from the ranch complex. Others picked up on their intention and joined in the effort.

RILEY AND PLÁCIDO HURRIED INTO the yard and stopped just shy of the well near the corral. Riley looked around. "We need buckets."

"*Sí*, the barn."

They moved quickly to the barn. Plácido tugged the door open, and both men bounded in. Riley stopped dead at the sight of the two lighted lamps hanging on pillars. He scanned the area, settling on the figure of a man near the open back door, swiping a large branch across the floor. "Hey, who the hell're you?"

Rawls stopped, dropping the branch as Riley and Plácido advanced on him.

Plácido shouted. "What you do *aquí?*"

Rawls's eyes darted between the two as they approached. His hand shifted to his holster, pulling the Army .44. Without hesitation, he fired from the hip, hitting Riley in the left arm. The ranch hand hollered and grabbed at the wound as the slug spun him. He dropped to his side.

Plácido, bulkier and slower than Riley, darted to his right, reaching for a nearby pitchfork. He turned and made a run at Rawls. A second shot from the Colt put a ball into Plácido's ample stomach. He doubled over and cried out, then dropped in a heap at Rawls's feet.

Almost in a panic, Rawls turned on his heels and bounded out the back door.

Riley forced himself up and staggered to his friend. "Plácido!" He took a knee beside the man. *"Plácido!"*

"HEAR THAT? SOUNDED LIKE SHOTS." Shawnee strained to

hear as he straightened from beating the blanket on the brush to stamp out embers.

Cletus looked around and reacted almost as an afterthought. "Yeah, it did."

Terry leaned toward them. "We got this."

The fire was mostly smoking remnants, having lost the fight with the Tell riders.

Shawnee moved first. Cletus followed. Both headed at a trot into the yard, noticing at the same time the open barn door. As they approached, the bunkhouse door opened, and Chrissie came out carrying a pistol along her leg, pointed at the ground.

She stopped at the sight of them. "I heard two shots. I'm sure of it."

Shawnee nodded but kept going toward the barn. "Heard 'em, too."

Cletus broke off and stopped in front of Chrissie. "You best stay put till we check this."

"No, I—"

"I ain't arguing this with you. Just do like I says. And put that gun down." He turned quickly and followed Shawnee into the barn.

In the low light thrown by the two coal oil lanterns, Riley knelt at Plácido's body, holding his arm as blood oozed through his fingers. They rushed to him.

Cletus took a knee at Riley and went right to tending the man's wound. "What happened?"

Shawnee crossed to the other side of the body and crouched to check for life signs. He looked up and shook his head as Riley spoke.

"We come in to get buckets. Seen this hombre near the back door. We called him out. Then he pulled iron and shot me. Time I got m' wits back, he'd plugged Plácido. I think he's dead."

Shawnee nodded. "He's dead."

They looked around. Every stall was empty.

Cletus's face scrunched. "Son of a bitch. They run our horses off."

Shawnee got up and went to Gray's stall. The signs of the struggle were evident. They got him, but he gave as good as he got. He moved quickly to the back door, taking note of the branch. Trying to scratch out the signs. He stopped and crouched at the doorway. Tracks could be seen in the negligible light, but they were there. He rose as Chrissie entered by the front door and stopped short at the sight of violence.

"Oh, God, what happened?" She still held the revolver.

Cletus got up and went to her, trying to shield her from what she'd already seen. "Now, Chrissie, we gots a sit-chi-ation we gots to deal with, and you being here ain't helping." He pulled the gun from her hand. "Now, please go back to the house. It safe now."

Chrissie stood her ground. "You've got to stop treating me like a child. I'm not going to go hide in the house. I'm part of this. I want to do whatever I can to help."

Cletus stopped in his tracks as Shawnee joined them. Cletus hauled in a breath. "I reckon you be right, girl. You your father's daughter. I'll respect that. What happen here, some scoundrels done run off our horses. They plugged Riley and done killed Plácido. We in big trouble here."

Chrissie took a second, then engaged. "First things first. How bad is Riley?" She moved toward him as Riley answered up. "Ain't that bad, ma'am. Hurts like the devil, but it won't do me in."

She crouched next to him. "Let me see."

Cletus stared in admiration at the girl.

Behind them, Terry and Cookie entered the barn from the yard. Terry went to Cletus. "Fire's out."

Without a word, Cookie went directly to where Chrissie tended Riley. "What we got?"

Cletus filled Terry in. "Horses is gone. Plácido's dead."

Terry frowned as he scanned the empty stalls. "Shit."

Shawnee joined them. "Might as well see to what we can get done tonight. Can't track horses in the dark."

11

AFTER RILEY'S WOUND WAS BOUND up and Plácido's body was buried in a shallow grave near the Tell complex, sleep came in varying forms to the different members of the small Tell community. While most of the hands, exhausted by the intensity and physical demands of beating down the brush fire, slept soundly, Shawnee, Cletus, and Chrissie did not.

Restlessness due to concerns for the future of the ranch caused Cletus, in the bunkhouse, and Chrissie, alone in her room, to toss and turn. Neither secured the rest that was sought and so badly needed.

Shawnee, fearing for Gray's safety, lay completely awake, waiting for the first rays of dawn when light could facilitate tracking. As soon as night dissipated, he was up and out. First checking the interior of the barn, but finding nothing new, he crouched at the rear doorway to examine the hoof prints and footprints left by the illicit activity. Careful not to trample anything that could help, he at least determined the direction taken by the thieves. As he returned to the barn, he found Cletus entering from the front.

"Couldn't sleep neither, huh?" Cletus joined him in the center of the barn.

Shawnee shook his head. "They got Gray. I ain't resting till he's safe."

"I know how you feel, but if they scattered them horses, they likely find their way back home, Gray included."

"No chance they just scattered 'em. Anybody goes to the trouble of sneaking 'em out the back like they done, they got a plan, and it don't include us getting 'em back."

Cletus nodded slowly. "Yeah. They knows we can't work cattle without 'em, and I got an idea who's behind this."

Shawnee picked up on that thought. "Cade Bynum."

"Yeah, Bynum." Cletus made a fist and pushed it against his open hand. "Son of a b—" He caught himself before the curse came out fully as Chrissie appeared in the doorway.

The girl was a sight in a wrinkled blouse and what appeared to be a pair of her father's range pants rolled up at the ankles and belted into folds at the waist. Her hair was pulled up under a wide brim hat.

Shawnee noted at how, as disheveled as she was, she was still a natural beauty. He bit his tongue to halt his tendency to tell her.

She approached them. "Have you found anything new?"

Shawnee gestured a thumb toward the rear of the building. "They's fresh tracks outside, but by now they might could be a good piece away. We got to ring in some more horses fore we can run 'em down. Know of any mustangers in these parts?"

Cletus answered up. "Nope. Closest horses is over to Dallas, and they ain't cheap. Last I knowed, they was close to fifty a head."

"Then we'll have to get the money from the bank," Chrissie said. "They're running this operation now. They should want to keep it going, so they should be willing to let us buy horses."

Cletus nodded. "Reckon we going to find out. You ready for a long walk to Fort Worth?"

A determined look crossed Chrissie's face. "Yeah, I'm ready."

Shawnee turned toward the back door. "I'm going to follow

them tracks some, at least maybe cipher the direction they took." He hurried out.

After a short distance, the trail petered out in hard, rocky ground. Frustrated, he returned as Chrissie and Cletus prepared for their journey to Fort Worth.

Cletus finished filling canteens as Shawnee approached. "You find anything?"

"Trail went cold in some rocks. Best I can cipher, they're heading southwest. Lot of country out there."

Cookie stepped out of the cook shack with a parcel wrapped in a cloth. He handed it to Chrissie. "Ain't much. Just some pemmican, but it'll keep you going."

Cletus capped the canteen. "Time we got to hoofing."

Shawnee looked southwest. "While you do that, I'll see if I can pick up that trail again. They ain't holding onto Gray without a fight."

AFTER A THREE HOUR HIKE, Chrissie and Cletus entered Fort Worth. Having paced themselves, consumed the food Cookie had provided, and kept themselves hydrated, they were tired but not exhausted. Their first stop was the doctor's office to send Dr. Ramsey to the Tell for Riley.

Cletus waited outside while Chrissie entered.

As she closed the door, Dr. Ramsey entered from the examination room. He stopped short at seeing Chrissie. "Why, Miss Tell, good morning." His gaze took in her ill-fitting and distinctly unfeminine clothes and noted her haggard, frowning expression as well. That did not concern her.

"I'm afraid it's not such a good morning, Doctor. We had some trouble at the Tell last night. One of our hands, Cliff Riley, was wounded. I need you to go out to tend to him."

Ramsey was instantly engaged. "How serious is it?"

"He was shot in the arm. Our cook cleaned and bandaged it, but I'd feel better if he has professional attention."

He nodded. "Of course, of course. I'll leave straight away after I finish with the patient inside." He indicated the examination room. "A few moments at most."

"Thank you." Chrissie turned for the front door.

"Miss Tell."

She stopped and turned.

The doctor fidgeted for a second before speaking. "Forgive me. I know this is a most inopportune time, particularly with the passing of your father, but would you consider...? I mean, may I...?" He trailed off in mid-sentence.

Chrissie waited a beat. "Doctor?"

"I'm so sorry. I should not have...." Again he hesitated.

"No, please. What did you want to ask?"

His face took on a determined look. "If I may... well, call on you at some point."

Then it was Chrissie who hesitated.

Oh, my! He's... interested in seeing me.

She collected herself. "I'm flattered, Doctor, really I am. But I'm afraid with everything that's going on... this is not a good time."

He took a breath. "I quite understand. I apologize for intruding on your grief. It was inconsiderate on my part. Please forgive a fool if you would."

Chrissie smiled. "There's nothing to forgive, Doctor. Perhaps another time."

"Of course." He glanced over his shoulder at the exam room

door and began backing toward it. "I should... see to my patient." He turned and quickly stepped into the room.

Chrissie stood there for a long moment, pondering the event. As flattering as the doctor's attention was, should she even consider pursuing it, or allowing him to do so, when her true interest was Shawnee? This was not the time to think about that. She went to the door and exited to find Cletus waiting.

He picked up on her demeanor. "Something wrong?"

Preoccupied, Chrissie hesitated. "What? Oh, eh, no, nothing wrong. He'll go in a few minutes. I need to see that banker."

Then they moved on to the bank. Cletus stopped as Chrissie approached the door. "Best I wait out here. No need my color causing more problems."

Chrissie nodded and entered the bank. Her knock on the office door brought permission to enter from Manion. She stepped inside to find Manion seated at his desk.

He rose as she approached. "Good morning, Miss Tell. What can I do for you?"

Without Manion's invitation, Chrissie occupied one of the chairs, sitting heavily, reflecting her weariness. She huffed out a breath. "I'm afraid I need your help."

Manion smiled. "Yes, of course, if I can."

"The ranch was raided last night. One of our men was killed, another wounded, and all our horses were stolen."

Manion seemed surprised at the development. "Why, that's terrible. Do you think you'll be able to locate the horses?"

"We can't count on that. It'll take some time to track them down. And we'll need horses to do that and to run the ranch as well."

"Yes, I realize that. How will you do that?"

Chrissie leaned forward, placing her forearms on the edge of the desk. She spoke slowly, carefully, to illustrate the gravity of the situation. "I need the bank to advance me the money to buy horses."

Manion appeared to think it over. He shook his head. "I'm sorry, Miss Tell, I can't. The Tell has been operating at a loss for some time now. I'm doing everything I can to turn it around, but an outlay like that at this time is just not possible. I'm told that horses are going for upwards of fifty dollars a head. I'm sorry, but I'm not at liberty to risk the bank's funds on an expenditure that promises to show no return on investment."

Chrissie reacted strongly. "Wait a minute. What are you saying? The Tell has always been profitable. How is it suddenly operating at a loss?"

"I'm afraid your father was not the businessman we all thought he was. I'll gladly show you the books if you don't believe me. Figures don't lie."

Dejected, Chrissie sat back. "I didn't say it was a lie. I just find it hard to believe."

"I'm sure you do. Hearing something as disheartening as this is not easy to accept, but I'm afraid my hands are tied. We'll just be able to make this month's payroll." He raised his hands in a futile gesture.

Chrissie thought quickly. "What about my personal funds? I can withdraw what we'll need. There must be enough in the account."

Manion shook his head. "No doubt there is, but that's not the problem. I can't authorize a withdrawal without permission. The agreement your father signed made Mister Bremmer your guardian. He has control over all your assets. You'd have to get his permission for a withdrawal of any amount."

Now frustrated, Chrissie got up abruptly. "All right, Mister Manion. If that's how it is, I'll see Mister Bremmer." She turned on her heels and stormed out, slamming the door behind her.

Cletus reacted to her frustration as she joined him on the board-walk. "No good?"

She shook her head. "He said he can't. Some nonsense about the Tell losing money."

Cletus looked confused. "What?"

She nodded. "Yeah. Operating at a loss, he called it."

"That don't sound right."

"Damn right it doesn't. I don't know that I believe him, but we don't have time right now. I've got to see Bremmer to get money from my personal account. I need to see him now."

"Son of a b— Damned if he didn't just lock up his place and head east out a town."

More frustrated, Chrissie's eyes went skyward. "Damn." She took a breath. "Well, I guess we leave that for another time. We should start hiking home."

"Let's get us a rig from Old Ed. Beats walking."

"Yes, it does. I guess the Tell can at least cover that."

They set out for the livery.

A SHORT TIME LATER, IN a one horse buggy, they came up the road leading into the ranch complex. Cletus pulled up near the barn as they observed the Tell hands seated and standing around the bunk-house door. Chrissie, spotting Shawnee with the group, climbed out of the rig and hurried toward him.

"Did you find any sign?"

Shawnee shook his head. "Tracked 'em to some rocks a ways out. Need a four legged critter to get through 'em. How'd you make out?"

Cletus joined Chrissie as she spoke. "Nothing from the bank. I did find out the Tell is losing money, although I'm still not sure I believe that. I've got money in my personal account, but I can't touch it without *permission* from Bremmer."

Cletus chimed in. "Yeah, and he just rode out a town."

Chrissie finished her thought. "So, stymied at every turn."

Shawnee made a face. "You get the feeling ain't none a this happening by chance?"

Cletus piped up. "*I* sure do."

Chrissie turned away. "I'm not even sure my account has enough for all the horses we need."

Shawnee leaned up against a porch pillar. "Anybody in these parts run mules?"

Chrissie and Cletus shot looks at him that seemed to indicate he might have lost his mind.

Cletus pushed his hat back. "Mules?"

"Yeah, I ain't *loco*. They's some ranches I worked that uses mules in tough country. They got better footing than horses. And they're cheaper to buy and keep."

Chrissie's interest was piqued. "How much cheaper?"

"A heap, I'd say."

Cletus nodded. "Well, they's a freighter just outside a Fort Worth. Runs mules to haul his wagons. Mister Tell staked him a while back. Purlee... no, Purlow's his name, as I recollect. Maybe we get some of his mules."

"Worth a try," Shawnee said.

"How about I go see Mister Purlow, see if I can strike a deal?"

Chrissie perked up. "Go ahead. And check if Bremmer came back. Maybe we've still got a chance."

12

CLETUS DROVE THE BUGGY THE length of Main Street, passing the last building in the town. He covered several yards of empty ground, continuing toward a large, one-story, log structure situated on the left side of the road. In its center, a double door large enough to fit a full-sized Conestoga wagon was fully open. Above it, in large black painted lettering, a sign stated *Purlow Freighters, Miles Purlow, Owner*. To the right of the opening was a small, man-sized door over which a smaller sign read *Office*. Cletus headed for that entrance.

As he entered, a loud voice from inside the building sounded. "Get them mules hitched up and get moving, dammit. You behind schedule." The voice had a southern twang and a clarion quality that allowed it to be heard throughout the entire structure. Cletus walked to the table.

The office was only large enough for the wooden table and chair set against the far wall. Tacked to the wall, a blackboard had a listing of shipments scrawled on it in white chalk. Several of the listings had lines drawn through them. Others did not. To the left of the wall, a small opening without a door led into the vast interior. Cletus digested the scene while he waited.

In a few seconds, the owner of the voice entered through the open doorway and called over his shoulder into the warehouse. "Set up the Dallas run next." He was tall and skinny with a long, gaunt face and a prominent nose. Several days of gray beard growth covered his lower face. A coonskin hat sat on his head, and a buckskin jacket was open on his shoulders. He stopped short at the sight of Cletus. "Oh, howdy there, friend."

"How do. You Mister Purlow?"

"Mighty well told I be. What can I do you for?"

"Name's Cletus Workman. I the foreman over to the Tell Ranch."

Purlow went to the table, putting it between himself and Cletus. "Oh, yeah, Bruno Tell's outfit. Sure a damn shame he passed. He was a good man."

Cletus nodded. "He was that. I come needing help for the Tell."

"Need something hauled, do you?"

"We need some mules."

Purlow's eyes narrowed. "Mules? What for you need mules?"

"Well, sir, it's a long story."

"Let me tell you something, friend. I'm a busy man here. Only reason I'm giving you the time of day is 'cause you're from the Tell. Hadn't been for Bruno Tell, I wouldn't be standing here right now. He staked me when wouldn't nobody else would, so I'm well-disposed to listen to you. But I got a business to run here, so I'd be obliged if'n you give me the short of it."

"Short of it, somebody done run off our cow ponies, every last one of 'em. We can't afford to replace 'em. We hoping to get some mules instead."

Purlow's look became intense. "Sounds like some damn body got a mad on for you folks."

"Seem like."

"Well, now, that ain't nice. Ain't even friendly. I reckon you're looking to use them mules to work your cattle?"

"Yes, sir."

"Heard tell of that being did. Mules'll have to be trained, but yeah, that'd work. How many you reckon you'll need?"

"Twenty-odd should ought to do it."

Purlow pondered this for a long moment. "Seeing as how I'm beholden to Tell, take 'em for twenty a head. That be the cost I pays to replace 'em."

Cletus did some quick mental calculating. "I ciphers that to be four hundred."

"Key-rect. And I'll help you train 'em as well, no charge."

Cletus smiled. "That be mighty decent of you."

"Least I can do. Well, now, friend, you come on back with the dee-nero, and we got us a deal."

"I be back in a spell." Cletus turned to leave.

"I'll be here."

Cletus's drive back to the center of Fort Worth put him in close proximity with Bremmer's office. A horse stood at the hitch rail. He slowed the rig to peer into the office. There was a figure inside. Taking it to be Bremmer, he snapped the reins on the rig horse, heading out of town at a trot.

CLETUS HAD THE HORSE AT a gallop as the buggy barreled into the Tell yard. He hauled back on the reins as Chrissie, Shawnee, and the Tell riders crowded around him.

Chrissie stood next to the carriage, wringing her hands. "Did you talk to Mister Purlow?"

"Surely did. He'll give us what we need, and he'll help train 'em. Four hundred."

"That's better than I'd hoped for." A smile crossed her face. "Now I just have to see my guardian for the money. Then we can go get the mules."

A cheer went up from the men as Cletus climbed out of the rig, and Chrissie climbed in.

"I'd just as leave you go ahead on alone. That man and me, we don't zactly see eye to eye."

Chrissie picked up the reins. "It's all right. This part's up to me. I'll handle it." She snapped the reins and turned the buggy to head it back to Fort Worth.

AS CHRISSIE DROVE THE STREET toward Bremmer's office, she contemplated her next move in this forced chess game. In truth, Shawnee's idea of mules seemed farfetched, but she knew he wouldn't propose something that was unworkable. So, her presentation to Bremmer would be that mules would cost much less, effectively saving money for the ranch. She reined up, climbed down, and, without knocking, went in.

Bremmer looked up from his desk and flashed a smile that looked forced. "Why, good day, Miss Tell. What brings you to Fort Worth?"

Chrissie moved forward to the desk. "Mister Bremmer, I can't believe I'm saying this, but I have to ask you to authorize a withdrawal from my personal bank account. Mister Manion won't allow it on my say so alone."

Bremmer thought for a second. "Yes, according to the guardianship agreement, he's absolutely right."

Chrissie breathed an impatient sigh. Though necessary, she found the continuation of this exchange tedious and tiresome. It came across in her statement. "I need you to authorize it."

"Well, I need more information before I can do that."

Now anger rose in Chrissie. "What do you need?" This came out quite short.

"I need to know how much you need and what the purpose of the withdrawal is."

Chrissie's lips tightened. "I need to buy some mules. Our horses were run off yesterday, stolen. We intend to use the mules to work the cattle and to locate our horses, but Manion won't advance the money. He says the ranch is doing badly and can't afford anything but the payroll. I'm going to pay for the mules from my account."

"I see. And how much are these mules going to cost?"

"Four hundred." She lost more of her patience. "Just authorize the withdrawal. I'm sure I have enough to cover it."

Bremmer sat back. "My dear girl, I can't just allow you to spend your money on some pie-in-the-sky scheme that might or might not work. I wouldn't be doing my job as your guardian if I did that. I'm charged with protecting your assets. Now, if the ranch is in trouble, that's Mister Manion's responsibility to rectify, not yours. I'm sure he's doing everything he can."

Chrissie's anger and frustration increased. "Don't patronize me, Mister Bremmer. This guardian thing might have been my father's idea, but it certainly is not something I agreed to. The Tell is my responsibility. I'm quite capable of making informed decisions. I'm not trusting the Tell's survival to anyone else, especially someone like Manion. Frankly, I don't trust him."

Bremmer raised his hands in a calming gesture. "Please. I can see you're upset. That was not my intention. I want only the best for you."

Chrissie was resolute. "Then allow the withdrawal."

Bremmer paused, again appearing to ponder. "I cannot. However, what I can and will do is loan you the amount you need. The loan will be made to you but will become the responsibility of the ranch. I'll word the agreement that way. It can be paid back at such time as Mister Manion determines is feasible. It allows you to discharge the responsibility you feel you owe the ranch at no personal expense, while it allows me to adhere to the guidelines of the guardianship agreement. Now, how does that sound to you?"

Chrissie stopped to think. On its face, the proposal seemed as though it would work, and although she was suspicious of Bremmer overall, she could not immediately determine an ulterior motive behind the offer. The decision needed to be made quickly, though, so without questioning it any further, she acquiesced. "Yes, I suppose that will work."

Bremmer smiled broadly. "Excellent. Give me a moment to draw up a quick loan agreement, then I'll get you the cash."

While Chrissie stood by, Bremmer hurriedly scrawled out a one page document, then turned it for her to read and sign. He opened the safe behind him and got up with cash in hand. He counted out the four hundred into her hand. "There you are. Just as promised."

Still digesting this, Chrissie spoke quietly. "Thank you."

Bremmer's smile broadened. "You are quite welcome."

"Mister Bremmer, I think I—"

He finished her statement. "Misjudged me? It's quite understandable. Being told what to do by someone you hardly know can be disconcerting. I hope you'll come to see that I only have your best interests at heart."

Chrissie smiled sheepishly. "I hope so, too." Feeling still somewhat uncertain as to Bremmer's voracity, she went to the door and left.

UPON CHRISSIE'S EXIT, BREMMER SHOOK his head in wonder and smirked. Mules! What folly! Leaving the office, he crossed to the bank and went to the rear of the building. He used his key to enter Manion's back door.

Bynum, seated in Manion's guest chair, looked around as Manion's attention went to Bremmer's entrance. The grin on Bremmer's face seemed to pique their interest.

"I want you both to hear this." He stopped to chuckle. "It's rich."

Manion and Bynum showed attention, but they said nothing as Bremmer took a seat.

"I, or rather the bank, just loaned Christina Tell four hundred dollars, another step in our takeover of the Tell. But the best part is the reason for the loan. It seems someone ran all their horses off, and she wants to replace them... with *mules.* Can you believe that?"

Manion laughed with Bremmer, but Bynum was not moved.

"That ain't so farfetched." Bynum's reaction stopped the laughter cold. Bremmer and Manion looked at him inquisitively.

Bremmer engaged immediately. "What do you mean?"

"I worked a couple ranches that used mules, mostly in the foothills. Worked out fine."

"Are you saying it's possible to work cattle with mules?" Bremmer was amazed.

"I seen it done. Mules ain't so dumb as they look. Reckon you got skunked, partner."

Bremmer's initial reaction was embarrassment. "Shut up, Bynum."

Bynum raised his hands in a shrugging gesture. "Hey, happens to the best of us."

Bremmer bit his lip. "Son of a bitch!"

Bynum spoke again. "Reckon them Tells ain't so dumb, neither."

"I said shut up!" Bremmer tugged at his goatee. "All right. We'll have to come up with something to turn this our way."

SHAWNEE STEPPED OUT OF THE bunkhouse as a cloud of dust appeared in the distance on the road coming in from Fort Worth. He stopped out of curiosity to determine what caused the disturbance. A herd of better than a dozen mules came into view. The lanky man on the saddled mule who rode point seemed out of place on the smaller animal, his height better suited to a horse. As the mules approached under the dust, Chrissie could be seen driving the carriage alongside the pack.

Shawnee crossed to the corral and opened the swing gate in preparation to enclose the mules. He waited at the gate. Purlow rode straight into the corral, leading the mules in with him. Chrissie split from the group and stopped the rig near the corral. Turning at the far end of the corral, Purlow directed his mount around the mules and along the fence to the opening. As he approached it, Shawnee closed the gate to the point of fitting only the rider through. When Purlow was outside, Shawnee closed the gate completely and looped its securing rope around the fence post to lock it in place.

"Thank you kindly." Purlow dismounted.

Chrissie climbed down from the buggy. Cletus joined her, and they went to where Shawnee and Purlow stood.

"Shawnee," Cletus said. "This here's Mister Purlow. He done sold us them mules."

Shawnee shook hands with Purlow. They exchanged greetings.

"Just call me Muley. Reckon you can see why."

By now, the Tell cowboys came out of the bunkhouse to crowd around. Cletus introduced Purlow to them. "He going to learn you how to handle them mules."

Purlow took the cowhands in tow and brought them into the corral to familiarize them with their replacement mounts.

Shawnee walked toward the barn, approaching Chrissie. She stopped him. "Any sign of the horses?"

"Trail turns west but nothing more. I'm going to saddle one a them mules and head back out. I can cover more ground riding."

"I'm coming with you. I'll take the buggy horse."

"Now, Chrissie, that ain't such a good idea. I find them horses, I'll likely find the horse thieves as well, and things might could get a tad ugly."

"There's nothing I can do here. If we do find the horses, you can stay and watch them while I get help."

Shawnee pondered for a second. "I reckon, but you got to do what I tell you, hear?"

"Yes, sir." She smiled.

Shawnee shook his head as he continued into the barn to fetch his saddle. When he came out, Chrissie was already detaching the rigging to free the horse. He continued on to the corral to select a mule as Chrissie led the horse into the barn. By the time he'd saddled a mule, Chrissie emerged ready to ride. They mounted. He turned west and moved out. Chrissie fell in behind him. They rode quickly, covering the ground Shawnee had already traveled on foot. Once he picked up the trail, Shawnee slowed the pace to better scrutinize for signs of the horses.

They tracked until midafternoon. Shawnee glanced at the position of the sun. "Ain't a whole heap of daylight left. We'll keep going till we run out."

"What do you think is going on? Why is somebody trying to cripple the Tell? And who do you think that might be?"

"Not sure, but I ain't the biggest admirer of that banker fellow. Strikes me he be more'n a tad slippery."

"What do you think he's up to?"

"Ain't ciphered that part out yet. I'll get there, though. Just a matter of time."

They kept moving west, following what Shawnee termed a possible trail. As the sun waned, sighting the markings became difficult.

"Getting tough to read sign. We ought to head back."

"Do you mind if we stop for a while first?"

"We can get down and stretch a mite."

They pulled up and dismounted, holding their reins. Shawnee stared at the country to the west, wondering just where the hell Gray and the other horses were being held. He stood there for a long moment.

"You miss him, don't you?" Chrissie said. "Gray, I mean."

"More'n I can say."

Chrissie moved to his side. "That's kind of how I felt when you didn't come back from that drive, all those years ago."

Shawnee looked at her, a confused expression on his dust-caked face. "How's that?"

"Well, Gray is more than a friend to you. I thought of you as more than just a friend back then. I had feelings for you. I think I still do."

"Now, Chrissie, you can't be doing that. You don't want to get mixed up in my kind a life. That ain't no place for a woman."

"So, you do think of me as a woman."

"Course I do. You're a fine woman. It's just—"

"But you don't feel that way about me?"

Shawnee saw where this was going. Why was she playing this game? He knew he had to shut it down. "That ain't what I'm saying. Look, I been running since I's sixteen, running from other folks, running from the law, and that ain't letting up. Ever. I'd never ask a woman to live like that. It ain't fair, and I won't do it."

"Oh!" Chrissie turned away.

Shawnee guessed he could have said that more gently. "Look, Chrissie, I didn't mean to upset you. I think too much of you to let you become an outlaw's woman 'cause that's what I am, an outlaw, a hunted man. They's lawmen and bounty hunters all over this country trying to run me down. Even that state officer you got in Fort Worth's got a notion he seen me somewheres. Won't be long 'fore he puts it together and I wind up running again. What kind a man would I be, I ask a woman to side me in that?"

Chrissie turned to face him. Tears ran down her cheeks. She sniffed and took a breath. "What about me? What about what *I* want? It's been four years. I'm grown now. I know my own mind. We could find a way. There's always a way, isn't there?"

"Ain't nothing I'd like better'n to be with you. But there ain't no way, not for us. I can't."

"Can't or *won't?*"

"Can't. I... Chrissie, I love you too much to do that to you. You got to see that."

She shook her head. "All I see is you rejecting me. We could find a way."

"No, and I ain't rejecting you. I'm keeping you from making a mistake that'll ruin your life. You're going to make some decent man a good wife someday. I ain't standing in the way of that happening."

She wiped tears away and looked him in the eye for a long moment. Her voice cracked. "I know." She leaned in and kissed him on the cheek. He felt the wetness of her tears on his skin, but this kiss was different. It seemed to come more out of respect than love.

"I love you for that. And I always will." She leaned away.

He whispered as he turned to remount. "I'm really sorry."

"Shawnee."

He stopped and turned toward her as she spoke.

"You're a better man than you let on to be."

13

ABOUT FIVE MILES WEST OF the point at which Shawnee and Chrissie broke off their search, in a secluded ravine, nineteen horses grazed quietly while Gray, several yards from the herd, kept watch over them. At the crest of the hill, Pete Rawls sat at a cold campsite with a rifle resting across his legs. He observed as his partner, Kaylo, a medium tall, stocky man in grimy trail clothes, approached Gray. A bullwhip was looped around the butt of Kaylo's sidearm. He carried a rope, held low and ready to toss.

When he was within a few feet of Gray, the horse backed up a couple steps. Kaylo continued, flipping the rope's loop back a little so it dragged on the ground. Gray stopped and stood his ground, whinnying defiantly.

Expecting trouble, Rawls got up and started down the slope, carrying the rifle. He reached level ground and continued into the herd since the straightest path to Gray was through them. The horses displaced as he walked, making way.

Kaylo closed on Gray as Gray whinnied again and reared on his hind legs. Hauling the rope up, Kaylo swung it above his head and let it go, aimed at Gray's head. At the same time, Gray came down on his front legs, causing the loop to miss. Before Kaylo could regain the rope, Gray moved forward, attacking. Within striking distance, the horse reared up and flailed his front hooves, closely missing Kaylo's head and chest. Kaylo pitched backward and sprawled on the ground, immediately rolling to avoid Gray's hooves as they stomped hard a few inches from his body.

Kaylo rolled over and grunted as he forced his feet under him. He pushed up to a standing position and uncurled his whip.

On the run now, Rawls moved closer, keeping the rifle ready.

Kaylo swung the lash straight at Gray's body. The resulting snap backed Gray up momentarily. Kaylo heaved the whip back and swung it again, grazing Gray's side. The horse made a painful sound as blood began oozing from the slash. Gray reared again, threatening both men. As his hooves hit the ground, Gray broke into a run straight at them, coming close enough to back them up. Before Kaylo could use the whip again, Gray changed direction and went to a gallop away from the area.

Kaylo dropped the whip and pulled his pistol. He took aim at the fleeing horse. Rawls stepped in and pushed Kaylo's arm toward the ground before he could cock the weapon.

"Quit that. You want to stampede the rest of 'em over one you can't break?"

"Ain't never seen the likes of that nag," Kaylo said through a thick southern drawl.

"I done told you he ain't having none, but no, you had to try."

"Never seen the horse I couldn't cowtow."

"Well, you just seen him, so let him go. What's one horse? We still got the rest of 'em."

They watched Gray run off at a gallop, leaving behind the threat of punishment.

DARKNESS ROLLED IN SLOWLY AS Cletus left the corral with Purlow. A good half day's work had accomplished the initial training of the mules and the indoctrination of the Tell cowboys into the handling of the animals. They walked to Purlow's waiting mule.

Purlow picked up the grounded reins. "I'll be back late morning, soon as I gets my runs set up. We can try the mules with some cattle, see how that works out."

"Well, we got more done than I 'spected. Thanks for your help."

"You betcha. Tell never hesitated when I needed help. I couldn't do no less."

Purlow mounted and directed his mule toward the main trail. As he moved, Cletus's gaze was pulled onto the road by the approach of two riders coming from the opposite direction. Purlow kept going, passing the riders as they entered the yard. Cletus's lips tightened. His eyes narrowed as he recognized the two. Manion and Bynum. What were they doing back here?

Purlow disappeared down the trail as Manion and Bynum pulled up near Cletus. They remained mounted.

Cletus directed his question to Manion. "What you want here?"

"Is Miss Tell here?"

"No, she ain't. Ain't sure when she'll be back, either, and you ain't welcome to wait, so you can just turn right around and ride the hell out of here."

Manion raised a calming hand. "Now, there's no call to act like that. I'm here on business."

Cletus stared intensely. "I don't much care why the hell you here. Miss Tell ain't here. That puts me in charge. I'm telling you leave. And you can take your muscle with you." He made a gesture of reference to Bynum.

Manion voice a protest. "Now, just a—"

Bynum cut him off. "You better shut your mouth, nigga."

Cletus took a threatening step. "I done told you stay off the Tell. Told you, you come back and they'd be guns a-waiting for you. Any part of that ain't clear to you?"

"You don't want to get into guns with me."

Shawnee's voice sounded behind Bynum. "Yeah, maybe he ain't that good." He paused, allowing the cocking of his revolver to be heard. "But I am."

Startled, Bynum attempted to turn in his saddle.

"You just keep on looking straight ahead, gunfighter. Touch that iron, it'll be the last you touch."

Cletus glanced past Manion and Bynum to see Chrissie siding Shawnee a few feet behind them. Both were mounted, and Shawnee pointed his gun straight on Bynum's back. Cletus smiled.

Manion broke in, raising his hand, palm out. "Look, we don't want any trouble. We'll leave and come back when Miss Tell is here."

Chrissie spoke up. "I'm right here, Mister Manion. What is it that you want?"

Manion looked straight ahead. "Well, I need to talk to you about the ranch."

Chrissie directed her horse forward and stopped alongside Manion. "I'm listening."

Manion turned in his saddle to face Chrissie. "I'm sorry to always bring you bad news, Miss Tell, but, unfortunately, I have more. I took another look at the books. The ranch is doing much worse than

I thought. I didn't realize until today that the taxes are due at the end of the month. There will only be enough funds available to cover salaries or the taxes, not both."

Cletus watched as the news hit Chrissie hard. She took a moment to grasp the gravity of it.

"Are you saying the ranch is failing?" Her voice was shaky.

"Unfortunately, yes. The next step would be bankruptcy."

Chrissie shook her head. "I don't understand. How is this possible? How could it have happened so fast?"

"Apparently it didn't. It's been happening over a long period of time. It seems your father ignored all the signs."

"I thought you knew what you were doing."

"I didn't ask for this responsibility. It was thrust upon me by your father. In truth, this is the first business of this kind that I've been asked to run. It's taken me some time to get oriented to its operation, but I now understand that the only way forward is to cut losses and cease operations."

Chrissie showed frustration. "Walk away from my father's life's work? I won't do that. I'll use my savings to keep it going."

"I anticipated you suggesting that. Before I came out here, I took the liberty of discussing that possibility with Mister Bremmer. He refused to let you bankrupt yourself in a futile effort to avoid the inevitable. He said he wouldn't be true to the guardianship agreement if he allowed it. There's also the loan he made to you. That would come due as part of the bankruptcy."

Shawnee broke in. "Surely sounds like you got it all wrapped up in a nice neat little package, mister banker. 'Most like it was planned that-a-way."

Manion craned his neck to see Shawnee as he spoke. "I resent that. I'm just trying to help here."

Cletus picked up on that. "Yeah, you helping us right off the Tell."

Manion returned his gaze to Chrissie. "Look, the bank is willing to take the ranch off your hands. We can offer you the amount covering the salaries, the taxes, and the loan as payment. Sign the Tell over to the bank, and we'll struggle with its future."

Shawnee nodded knowingly. "And there it is. Just like I ciphered. Squeeze the Tells out and buy it for a pittance."

Chrissie's anger erupted. "No! The Tell is *not* for sale, Mister Manion. Not at any price and definitely not at your price. You can take that offer and—"

Cletus cut her off, anticipating her descent into foul language. "You can get off the Tell." He drew his pistol. "Now." He moved to the side to keep Shawnee out of his line of fire.

Manion protested. "This is a mistake."

"Damn straight, it is. And you made it. Chrissie, you move away from 'em."

Chrissie turned her horse away a few feet and stopped.

Chewing his lip, Manion looked at Bynum, who remained in his same position.

Cletus took another step. "Time's a-wasting, gents. Git!"

Manion made the first move, turning his horse around. Bynum followed suit.

Shawnee kept his revolver trained on them as they passed. "Hey, gunsmith. One thing I can't abide's a horse thief. I find you had a hand in the thiefing a Tell horses, start looking over your shoulder. 'Cause I'll be coming for you."

Bynum did not respond. He just kept moving. Shawnee and Cletus kept their weapons ready until Manion and Bynum were far enough away to no longer pose a threat. Dismounting, Shawnee and Chrissie joined Cletus.

Cletus holstered his revolver. "Well, I reckon we done done it now. They'll likely have the law on us."

Shawnee shook his head. "No, they won't. They don't want the law anywheres near what they're doing."

"But we still have to find a way out of this," Chrissie said.

Shawnee looked off into the distance. "I got an idea about that. You recollect back when the war ended? They wasn't the army to buy Tell cattle no more. So, Mister Tell sent us on a drive to Kansas, and his beef set the market. What's to stop us from doing that again?"

"I recollect that, but we ain't got the horses we'd need for a drive. I doubt them mules can handle getting a herd to Kansas. They ain't even trained good enough yet to run down strays."

Shawnee faced Cletus. "Leave the horses to me. We got close today. I reckon one more day and I'll find 'em."

Chrissie, looking skyward, offered a thought. "Mister Grave, the Cattlemen's Association agent, he might have some ideas."

Cletus was skeptical. "What can he do?"

"I don't know, Cletus, but we need help wherever we can get it. Mister Grave knows the cattle business, and he was a good friend of Pa's. I'm sure he won't want to see the Tell fail. I'll go see him in the morning. I've got a feeling about this."

CHRISSIE GOT AN EARLY START in the morning, setting out for Fort Worth an hour after sunrise. The ride put her in the town about an hour before most businesses opened for the day, but she remembered Mr. Grave was an early bird, so she expected to find him in his office when she arrived. She'd accompanied her father on several visits he'd made to Grave. She was young enough to be disinterested in the business they discussed, but she did note all of their visits, as well as the kind and helpful nature of the man.

The Tarrant County Cattlemen's Association supported the ranchers in the county, seeking to standardize beef prices, to lobby for lower taxes, to facilitate joint cattle drives, and to provide assistance to members in need. Its office was located in Fort Worth since the town was also the county seat. For the past ten years, Asher Grave, former rancher and Texas freedom fighter, had been the local agent for the group. His office was located at the west end of Fort Worth in the second floor of a hardware store.

She rode down the main street as the sun burned off the last morning chill in the air. She stopped at the hitch rail in front of Marsden's Hardware and dismounted. The sign on the corner of the building caught her gaze. *Tarrant County Cattlemen's Assn., Asher Grave, Agent, Office Upstairs.* She rounded the corner and took the steps up to the second floor, stopping at the door. Her knock generated a call from a gravelly voice inside to enter. She opened the door and stepped in.

Across the small room, a pudgy man in a dark suit and tie sat behind an inexpensive wood desk. Even seated, he looked quite short. His face was round and had a pleasant expression. The lines in his face and his white, thinning hair gave evidence of his age. Chrissie guessed him to be close to seventy. She imagined the grandfather she never knew would look like Mr. Grave. This was the same thought she had when she first met him some ten years earlier. He looked up from his work.

"Good morning, Mister Grave." She flashed a cordial smile.

Grave's brow furrowed, and his eyes narrowed, as if he was pondering something. "I know you. I'm sure of it, but I can't—"

Chrissie thought to save him the work of remembering. "I'm Chrissie, Chrissie Tell, Bruno's daughter."

Grave's expression changed to wonder, then lit up in a smile. "Not little Chrissie. My, my, you're all grown up now. Come in, child, please, and sit you down."

Chrissie smiled back. She went to the chair that faced the desk and sat.

Grave frowned. "I was so sorry to hear about Bruno. I was away when it happened, but I went to his grave as soon as I heard. I'd have come by to visit, but I didn't want to intrude."

"I know you and Pa were good friends. I appreciate your thoughts."

"I've been hearing bits and pieces of what's going on with the Tell. None of it sounds good. Is there anything I—or the association—can do to help?"

"I hope so. It looks like we'll have to mount a drive to sell off enough cattle to pay the taxes and the hands. I can't believe the ranch is doing so badly. My father was a better businessman than that... at least I *thought* he was."

Grave leaned forward, resting his arms on the desk. "Chrissie, I *know* he was. I find that hard to believe."

"But Mister Manion says it's so, and I've no way of disputing him."

Grave's face showed anger. "Manion. That weasel. I never did like him. Always got an angle. He covers it well. Nothing definite, but some of the deals I've seen him involved in, they stank like a pig pen. And he always come out smelling like a rose." He shook his head. "How can I help you?"

"Our horses were stolen. We can't afford to replace them. The only way we can work cattle is with the mules Mister Purlow sold us, but he's still training them. We don't think they could handle a drive all the way to Kansas. Do you know of any drives nearby that we could join up with?"

Grave looked off toward the ceiling, then back at Chrissie.

"Actually, I do. There's a combined drive coming up from Waco. Should be here in a few days. They'll lay over outside of town to restock before moving on. You could hook your beeves up with them."

"Yes, that would work. I'm sure the mules can handle that without a problem. But there's something else. The taxes and the payroll are due at the end of the month. That only gives us about a week. How long will the drive take to reach Kansas?"

Grave gave that some thought. "Likely a good couple months, give or take."

Alarmed, Chrissie sucked in a breath. "Then it won't work. It'll be too late."

Grave went back to thinking again. "Supposing I was to, or let's say, supposing the *association* was to advance you the cash you need now. And you repay that when you get the money from the sale in Kansas. That should ought to settle things with that skunk, Manion."

"But if we don't make enough from the sale, then we owe you, as well."

Grave smiled at her. "How many head you sending?"

"About a thousand."

"And how much you need to square it with Manion?"

Chrissie took a moment to calculate. "Two thousand should do it."

"A thousand head at today's prices, that'll net you a good five thousand, maybe more. You got nothing to worry about 'cept getting out of Manion's clutches. And if you need help with that, you just let me know. I been itching to do him no good for quite a spell now."

Chrissie grinned broadly. "Oh, I could just kiss you."

Grave chuckled. "Now, now, no need to get carried away now. I'm just doing my job, protecting the county's ranchers." He got up and went to the small safe that rested on the floor behind the desk. For a few minutes, he fiddled with the safe combination, then he counted out the desired amount and dropped the coins into a small sack. He stepped around the desk and placed the bag in Chrissie's hand. "There you be, child. Two thousand dollars. I'll take care of the paperwork. Now don't you go paying off that Manion cuss till it's due, hear? He can wait. You get your beeves ready to go. I'll get word to you when the drive gets here, and I'll let them know you're joining up with them."

Chrissie got up, beaming. She leaned in and gave him a kiss on the cheek. "I can't thank you enough."

"Aw, that's all right. I can't wait to see the look on Manion's face when you pay him off. That'll be worth every penny."

Chrissie giggled and turned for the door.

"You keep fighting, Chrissie Tell, just like your pappy done."

14

UNDER PURLOW'S TUTELAGE, THE TELL cowboys and the mules they'd been paired with continued to learn. By now, the mules were comfortable with the saddles and the riders on their backs. They accepted direction without protest.

It was midmorning. A bright sun warmed the area with only a few clouds overhead. Outside the corral, Shawnee finished saddling his mule. The frown on his face told everyone where his mind was. For as many times as Gray had gotten him out of a jam, he owed it to the horse to find him and make sure he was safe.

As the hands saddled up in the corral, Cletus conferred with Purlow, then he announced to them that they would ride out to the north range to engage the mules with the cattle. He left the group and stepped out to join Shawnee.

"You heading back out to find the horses?"

"Yup."

"Good luck."

Shawnee nodded and prepared to mount. He stopped as he noticed Chrissie riding in from the main trail. He waited for her.

Cletus mounted and directed his mule from the corral toward the spot at which Chrissie drew rein. "How'd you make out?"

Chrissie had a smile on her face. "Better than I expected. Mister Grave not only told me that a drive coming up from Waco would be here in a few days, he advanced us the money we need to satisfy the bank against the sale of the cattle. All we have to do is drive the cattle to meet the herd outside Fort Worth. Once they sell the cattle, we can pay back the association."

"That'll be easy enough. We heading up the north range now to get the mules working some of the beeves. We can start the round-up while we there. We'll be ready." He turned his mule and rode to join the party heading north.

Shawnee mounted his mule and turned west.

Chrissie joined him. "Still trying to find the horses?"

"Got to. Gray's with 'em."

Chrissie looked past his shoulder. "Eh... no, he's not. Look." She pointed toward where her gaze was fixed.

Following Chrissie's finger, Shawnee saw a welcome sight. "Well, I'll be—"

Approaching quickly, the horse moved directly toward them. Shawnee dismounted and hurried to greet him. They came together a few feet away from Chrissie. Overcome with emotion, Shawnee reached out and hugged the horse's neck before he even came to a complete stop. Gray nickered appreciatively.

Shawnee stood back to examine his friend. At the sight of the mark of the the lash, he gritted his teeth. He patted Gray's forehead gently. "Sorry, boy, they treated you bad. They'll pay for that."

Chrissie rode the short distance to join them. "Do you think he can take us to the other horses?"

"I know he can, but first he needs some food and water. Then I'll patch him up." He turned and headed off toward the barn. "Come on, boy."

Gray followed.

Taking time to water the horse and strap on a feedbag full of oats, Shawnee put a healing salve on the whip wound and waited for him to finish the food. Only when he'd eaten every morsel did he lead Gray out of the barn to where Chrissie waited, still mounted.

Shawnee mounted the mule. "Gray, let's go find your friends. Go on, boy, find 'em."

Seeming to understand Shawnee's words, Gray moved forward a few yards, then looked back over his shoulder at them.

"Go on, boy." Shawnee spurred the mule forward. "We coming."

 Gray turned west and moved out while.

With Gray in the lead, they covered much of the same ground they had during their earlier search. By noon, they reached the spot where Shawnee and Chrissie had stopped to rest during the last trip. That made Shawnee more confident that he'd been on the right path to begin with. Gray stopped there and looked around. Shawnee guessed he was making sure of his bearings. The horse whinnied and nodded his head, then took out straight west at an even faster pace. Shawnee and Chrissie followed.

Riding hard for the next five miles, they approached an area of boulders high enough to shield whatever lay beyond them. Gray stopped and reared once. Shawnee and Chrissie rode in to join him.

"Way he's acting, I'd say we're close." Shawnee dismounted. Walking over to Gray, he patted the horse's nose. "Stay here, Chrissie. Let me check things out first."

Chrissie called out. "Be careful,"

"Yup." He moved forward on foot toward the outcropping of. Climbing up on the rocks, he tested his footing for safety as he went. Upon reaching the top, he stayed low and peered down a long slope. Halfway down, he saw a campsite on level ground. A small tent stood nearby. Outside the flap, two men lounged comfortably. Further down the continuing slope to where it straightened out, he saw the Tell horses grazing and milling around.

Pay dirt!

He pondered his next move. The horses had to be led to safety before he could throw down on the rustlers. He'd have to press Gray into service to lead the others away while he watched the outlaws. Once the remuda was out, those two *hombres* would be fair game. In truth, he hoped they'd put up a fight.

Hurrying back down the rocks, he went straight to Gray. "Found 'em, boy. Go get 'em. Now let's bring 'em out. Bring 'em here."

Gray looked at him for a moment, then nodded and nickered, seeming to understand.

"Go on, boy, go get 'em." He moved to Gray's rear and smacked the horse's hindquarters. "Go get 'em."

Gray cantered forward and around the boulders, disappearing from view.

Damn, but he's a smart one.

Shawnee pulled the Henry rifle from its saddle scabbard and turned back toward the rocks. "Stay here," he called over his shoulder to Chrissie. He again climbed to the top and looked down the hill.

The rustlers still lounged in the same spot.

Entering the depression from Shawnee's left, Gray galloped toward the herd, whinnying as he went. He circled, then stopped at the far end. Reared and whinnying, galloping first one way then another, he approached the remuda. Slowly at first, then with increasing urgency, the horses started toward the spot where Gray had appeared. Once they began to move, Gray again circled around the far edge of the herd to gain the lead.

Taken by surprise, the rustlers reacted, stood raised their rifles.

Shawnee shouldered the Henry, levered a round in place, and fired, kicking up dirt near Rawls's boot. He put another shot close to them before they turned their fire on him. Then they scattered to take cover behind some nearby rocks. Shawnee dropped to a prone position and expended the balance of the rifle's loads in an exchange of shots that either went wild or found marks in the rocks and dirt. He crawled over a few feet and brought his revolver into the fight.

Having emptied their rifles, Rawls and Kaylo pulled their side arms and continued the barrage.

As Shawnee fired his last revolver round, another weapon engaged the outlaws. Shawnee looked to his left to see Chrissie kneeling behind a boulder and firing her Winchester rifle down the slope. *Should a knowed she wouldn't stay put.* But she was in it now, and he sure could use the help. He counted two shots. She had twelve left. Shawnee took advantage of the time this gave him to reload the Henry. He waved to get Chrissie's attention.

He made a motion with his hand for her to slow down. He followed that with a shout. "Count your shots. Don't waste 'em. Just keep their heads down. I'm moving in."

She nodded, continuing sporadic fire. Shawnee rolled over twice, putting him further behind covering boulders. He rose and, crouching, went down the slope to a point where a rock offered cover.

Now on the rustlers' left, he opened fire. Chrissie joined in from her position, catching them in a crossfire.

Rawls and Kaylo stopped firing and stayed put. Uncertain if they were hit or out of ammunition, Shawnee held his fire. Chrissie followed suit. Then, with sudden moves, Rawls and Kaylo bolted down the slope to level ground and went to a dead run for the rocks on the far side of the ravine. Their move was enough of a surprise that both Shawnee and Chrissie missed a beat.

Seconds later, Shawnee recovered, firing two shots rapidly. The first kicked up dirt at Rawls's heels. The second hit Kaylo, knocking him down. Shawnee worked the lever on the Henry and checked the chamber. *Out. Shit. Lost count.* Distracted, he took his eyes off Rawls. A close shot from Rawls's rifle put him back behind cover. He shoved a single cartridge into the Henry's chamber and slammed the lever closed as he heard Chrissie's Winchester bark. When his eyes crested the boulder, Rawls was on the far side of the other side of the arroyo, climbing for all he was worth, and Kaylo scrambled for the rocks, holding his wounded arm. Shawnee fired his lone shot but missed. Now completely empty, with no time to reload, he growled his frustration as he watched them crest the ridge and disappear over it.

He turned back to Chrissie. "Break it off. Let 'em go."

Chrissie waved back and started climbing toward the crest of the hill. She went over the top and down the boulders toward her waiting horse. Shawnee followed her. When he reached her, Chrissie was engaged in reloading her rifle.

She looked at him with a grin. "How did I do?"

Shawnee nodded. "You done real good."

"I had a good teacher."

Shawnee reloaded as he spoke. "I learned you the Navy Colt. Who learned you the rifle?"

She shrugged. "Terry. He took me hunting after he taught me. I brought home an eight point buck."

Shawnee chuckled and nodded. "Good you learned. Now we got to round up them horses and get 'em back to the ranch."

As they mounted, Gray appeared a short distance away, leading the horse herd. Gray went directly to Shawnee. The herd stopped behind them.

"Good boy, Gray." Shawnee patted the horse's neck. "Let's get 'em home."

BREMMER LOOKED UP FROM HIS desk as Manion and Bynum entered his office. They stopped halfway to the desk and glanced at each other, saying nothing. Bremmer picked up on their uneasiness. "What the hell is wrong with you two?"

Still they hesitated.

Bremmer came to his feet. "Damn it, what the hell is going on? Come on. Out with it."

Manion swatted Bynum's arm. "Go on, tell him."

Bynum took a breath. "We lost the horses. The Tell found 'em and got away with 'em."

Bremmer's expression changed to a combination of surprise and anger. "Son of a bitch," he shouted, leaning forward on his fists. "What the hell, Bynum? You told me your men were competent. What happened?"

"I don't know. Something about a gray horse running the herd off. They lost their own nags , too, so I made 'em walk back for being so damn stupid."

Manion interrupted. "This damn fool is going to get us caught. He shows up at the bank and announces to everyone that the horses are gone."

"Shut up, both of you. Let me think." Bremmer sat heavily in his chair. His hand went to his chin as he thought. "Damn it! That gives them the chance I don't want them to have. If they get their affairs current, they'll set our plans back months. The longer we drag this out, the more we expose ourselves."

Bynum had a confused expression. "Come again?"

"Goddammit. Somebody's going to start asking questions we don't want asked."

Manion broke in. "We've got to do something quickly, Jarrett, before they can reorganize."

Bremmer came forward in his chair, elbows on the desk. "Tell me something I don't know." He paused in thought. "They'll probably try to arrange to sell off part of the herd."

"How do you know they'll try that?" Bynum asked.

Bremmer shot him a look that questioned his intelligence. "It's their only option to pay their bills."

"You think they'll try a drive north?"

"Yes, now that they have horses—no thanks to you."

Bynum shut up.

Bremmer sat back. "Enough of this. I'm through playing cat and mouse with them." He glared at Bynum. "You get every man you can find and stake them out between here and the Tell. They'll have to come east to get to a main trail going north. When they make their move, I want you ready. This time, don't stop until they're all dead."

"That'll stampede the beeves."

Bremmer came forward again. "Then, damn it, you'll round them up again. Now you listen to me, you son of a bitch, and you listen good. This is the last mistake I'll tolerate. I've got too much wrapped up in this to let you fumble your way around. Unless you want to lose your share in this, you damn well better do exactly what you're told without deviation. Do you understand me?"

Bynum fumed, but he held his anger. "Yeah."

Manion stepped forward. "Now, wait a minute, Jarrett. What you're suggesting is way outside the law. If that state officer gets wind of this and traces it back to us, we'll all end up in jail or worse."

"You wanted something done? Well, that's what we're doing. And don't worry about Malahide. He's not smart enough to put it together. Even if he does, by the time he does, Bynum and his men will be paid off and long gone. And we'll be as surprised by the whole thing as everyone else. I'm telling you, if we don't stop their progress now, we'll lose everything we've worked for."

Manion looked away. "There has to be another way. One within the law."

Bremmer slammed his hand on the desk loudly. "I'm running this, Manion. That's what I want done. Don't go against me. You won't survive it."

Manion let it go, letting out a heavy breath. "All right, never mind. I'm too deep in this now to think I can get out of it clean."

"That's being smart." Bremmer turned his attention to Bynum. "Get your men together and be ready to move fast. And this time, no slip-ups."

15

IN LATE AFTERNOON, GRAY STRODE proudly in front of the herd of Tell horses as they entered the ranch. Shawnee and Chrissie brought up the rear, keeping any strays from wandering. Gray stopped in the center of the yard. The other horses followed his lead, milling around him.

Shawnee glanced at the barn to see the door wide open. "Let's get 'em in the stalls."

He released the rope from its saddle tie and opened a loop. As he dropped the rope over the head of the nearest horse, Chrissie readied her rope. Together they led the horses one by one into the barn while Gray kept the rest of the herd in place.

When they had backed each horse into a stall, Chrissie did a count. "We have two extra horses."

Shawnee chuckled. "Likely belong to them owlhoots. Reckon they'll be walking a spell."

They filled feedbags and brought them out to the horses. As they emerged from the barn, Cookie stuck his head out of the cook shack. "That's a welcome sight right there. For sure and certain."

Shawnee joined Gray, still waiting outside the barn. "Let's get you some good oats, boy." They started back to the barn as Chrissie walked over to meet Cookie.

"How's Riley doing?"

"Doing fine, Miss Chrissie. Doc Ramsey was out this morning. Said I done a real good job patching him up."

"I'm glad to hear that."

"Me, too. Say, I got a fresh pot of stew ready, case you and Shawnee's feeling kind of hungryful."

"Well, I think Shawnee's kind of busy with Gray right now, but don't mind if I do."

Cookie opened the door and swung his arm toward the doorway. "Right this way, ma'am."

After her meal, Chrissie stepped out of the cook shack at the same time Shawnee exited the barn.

"How's Gray doing?"

"Be right as rain in a couple days. He's a tough one."

As they spoke, Cletus led the crew and Purlow in from the north range. The group stopped in the yard.

Cletus dismounted his mule. "How'd you make out tracking down our horses?"

Shawnee and Chrissie looked at each other and grinned.

"We got 'em all back," Shawnee said. "They all in the barn, safe and sound."

Cletus let out a whoop. "Well, that surely be good news. Mules'll do in a pinch, but they ain't cow ponies."

Purlow broke in. "Well, looks to be you ain't be need my mules after all. Just in case, though, why don't you hang onto 'em for a spell? When you're ready, bring 'em back and collect what you paid for 'em, even exchange. Ain't no rush."

Chrissie stepped forward. "Thank you, Mister Purlow. You've been more than helpful."

Purlow smiled. "I be proud to help the Tell, young lady. And you just call me Muley, like everybody do."

Chrissie smiled back.

Purlow turned his mule toward the main trail and rode out.

"Cletus," Chrissie said. "We need to get the trail herd picked out in the morning. We have to be ready when that Waco drive gets to Fort Worth."

"Right. We'll head out after breakfast. We started getting 'em cut out today, but like I said, mules ain't cow ponies. It'll be easier now we got horses."

Terry pointed toward the road coming in from Fort Worth. "We got company."

Driving a one horse buggy, Asher Grave pulled into the yard as all eyes turned his way. He drew rein close by. Chrissie hurried over to join him.

"Mister Grave, is something wrong?"

"I just got word from the trail boss. The drive up from Waco will be outside of Fort Worth in the morning. They're trying to make up time, so they're only staying long enough to lay in supplies. Can you get your herd to them tomorrow?"

Chrissie shook her head. "It doesn't look like we can. We just got our horses back. We've only begun the roundup."

Grave leaned toward her. "I'm sorry. The trail boss won't wait."

Chrissie turned away, her hand at the back of her neck indicating her frustration. Shawnee and Cletus closed on the rig.

Cletus went to Chrissie. "What's going on?"

"Mister Grave says the trail drive will only be in Fort Worth long enough to restock. They won't wait for us."

Cletus turned to Grave. "Can't you make 'em wait?"

Grave shook his head. "I don't have that kind of authority. The trail boss makes the rules."

Cletus turned away. "Damn it. We was so close. Even with good ponies, we can't get beeves rounded up and drove to town before they leave. 'Sides, we ain't got the remuda to make a drive to Kansas all by our lonesome."

Shawnee spoke up. "We might could pull this off if we round 'em up tonight and drive 'em straight through. We'd likely make it 'fore noon. It'll take 'em that long to stock up."

Cletus faced Shawnee with a look of disbelief. "You listening to what all you're saying? A night roundup? The boys're dog tired. Them horses ain't far behind. I don't see it working."

"It ain't so farfetched. Ain't like we got to brand 'em and all. We just cut out them we need and drive 'em straight to Fort Worth. Should be a full moon tonight, so we'll have the light. We got good horses and good wranglers. We can do it."

Cletus shook his head. Chrissie stepped between them. "As crazy as it sounds, I think it's possible." She nodded. "We can't just roll over without trying. I know Pa wouldn't. I say we try."

Cletus let out a breath. He turned to the hands who'd grouped near them. "You fellows up for some night work?"

A discussion followed for a few seconds. Then Terry stepped forward. "We with you, Miss Chrissie. We'll get us some grub and head out."

A cheer went up from the wranglers.

Chrissie grinned. "I guess you got your answer, Cletus. You're foreman. What do you say?"

Cletus shrugged. "Reckon Mister Tell'd turn over every stone. I can't do no less. Come on, boys, eat fast and saddle up."

OCCUPYING THE SAME SPOT HE had used earlier, Pete Rawls worked his spyglass to observe activities at the Tell. He watched the hands pile into the cook shack, then saddle up and head out. Only Chrissie and Cookie remained behind.

Rawls rode the main trail to Fort Worth quickly. When Bynum sent him on this mission, he advised him of the location of their camp, a site purposely chosen for its strategic position and its hidden location. As Rawls approached, Bynum stepped out from the bushes and waved him down.

"You got something to tell me?"

Rawls pulled up sharply a few feet away. "Yeah, some old geezer showed up, and they palavered with him a spell. Then they saddled up and headed out to the range. I got a wild notion they going to try to get a drive together tonight."

"Reckon they'll try anything." Bynum thought for a second. "They'll have to come east like Bremmer figures, and they got to pass through these parts. We'll nail 'em when they do." He waved his hand over his shoulder. "Head on into town and tell Bremmer about it."

That set Rawls off. "Why me? Shit, you got me riding all over creation. Why can't you send somebody else?"

Bynum shot back. " Cause I told *you* to go. Don't give me shit, Pete. You getting paid a heap more'n you're worth. Do what I damn well tell you."

Rawls boiled over. "Son of a bitch—"

"Cuss all you want, but you're going. Then get your ass back here. I want you working your glass to spot that herd a far piece out."

Rawls hesitated, cursed again, then slapped the reins on his horse's rump and headed for Fort Worth.

CHRISSIE EMERGED FROM THE MAIN house the next morning. She stopped on the porch and listened to the bawls of cattle in the distance. *Damn if they didn't do it.* She crossed quickly to the barn. A few minutes later, she exited, mounted, and struck out toward the location of the sounds at a gallop. She slowed as she approached the herd to prevent spooking the cattle, riding through them and pulling up near Cletus and Shawnee as they spotted her.

Both men pulled up and greeted her.

Cletus grinned. "Reckon ya'll was right. We done it."

"That's great. I'll ride the rest of the way with you."

Shawnee sided Chrissie. "I got a funny feeling you should ought to stay clear of this."

"I can't. I've got to be there to sign the herd over. I'm going."

"Well, at that, I reckon you got to, but I'll be keeping a eye on you."

Chrissie smiled. "I wouldn't have it any other way."

Shawnee chuckled.

Cletus made a circular motion over his head that could be seen by the riders stationed around the herd. "Point 'em east."

With a combined effort and much shouting, the cowboys turned the cattle and changed direction. Cletus, Shawnee, and Chrissie rode point to lead the way. Within a few seconds, the herd was at a slow but steady pace forward.

PERCHED ON A BOULDER ABOUT twenty feet above Bynum's camp, Pete Rawls used his spyglass to scan the area to the west. He'd been up here since returning from Fort Worth after delivering the message to Bremmer. So far, he'd seen nothing of interest, but from this vantage point, anything as big as a herd of cattle would be visible well in advance of its arrival. The flat plains of east Texas didn't hide much.

He'd hang here for another ten minutes or so. Then he'd be calling down for someone to relieve him. He needed some coffee and a lay-down for a spell. Another pair of eyes up here would be just as good as his, no matter what Bynum thought.

Then he saw it on his latest sweep of the countryside. It started as a wide column of dust rising on the open terrain between two outcroppings of odd shaped rocks that had to be a couple miles apart. He concentrated on the image, watching it as it moved east. After several minutes, forms were visible on the ground below the dust. A good sized herd moved toward his location. He waited another minute to verify what he saw, and in that time, he made out riders driving the beeves and keeping them bunched.

Rawls called to the camp. "Cade. They coming." He glanced down to see Bynum looking up at him.

Bynum waved at him. "Come on down."

Rawls moved to behind boulder and found the path he'd used to climb up. With carefully placed steps, he descended to level ground a few feet behind the campsite and trotted to where Bynum waited.

Bynum shouted at the group. "All right, saddle up. We moving."

The full complement of hired gunmen came to life. They moved quickly to their already saddled horses tied to a picket line strung between two mesquite trees.

Rawls joined Bynum. "How you want to do this? Spread out?"

"We'll do it like the cavalry. Fan out and charge 'em straight on. Them waddies is cowhands, they ain't gunsels. They see us coming on like that, they'll run 'fore they put up a fight."

"Hope you right." Rawls headed for his horse.

Bynum moved to his own mount. When the others were mounted, he and Rawls took the lead. Kaylo took a spot directly behind them.

Bynum called over his shoulder. "Let's do this, once and for good. Kill 'em all."

They moved out in a column to the west.

THE TELL HERD MOVED SLOWLY and steadily eastward. They entered an area that was bounded on both sides by mountainous regions separated by a flat plain that stretched about two miles across.

Dust rising in the east drew the attention of Shawnee and Cletus, riding point alongside Chrissie. Although about a mile away, the size of the cloud told Shawnee a good-sized group of horsemen were riding hard and headed straight for them. He glanced at Cletus but waited to give the alarm. Reaching into his saddlebag, he pulled out his spyglass to verify the threat. "We got company. Coming on fast."

"How many you see?" Cletus asked as they drew rein.

Shawnee lowered the glass. "Hard to tell. Hell of a lot more'n last time, though."

"I'll get the boys up here in front of the herd."

Shawnee thought for a second. "No, wait—put 'em behind the herd. When them waddies get close enough, stampede the beeves right at 'em. That should scatter 'em and give us a fighting chance."

"Let's do 'er. Come on."

They wheeled their horses and headed at high speed around the sides of the herd, Cletus taking one side and Shawnee, with Chrissie at his side, skirting around the other. As they reached the hands riding beside the cattle, they shouted at them to get to a position behind the drive.

"Stay together," Shawnee shouted as the cowboys grouped around him. "Follow my lead." He used the spyglass again to watch as the threat approached. This time, he recognized Bynum riding at the head of the group, along with that trigger-happy little fellow beside him. "That's Bynum leading 'em."

Satisfied at a quarter mile that they were close enough, he lowered the glass and drew his sidearm. "Stampede 'em! Run 'em down." He fired a shot in the air that startled the cattle and started them moving. Cletus and the Tell riders followed suit, firing in the air and taking off behind the herd.

Shawnee broke away to return to Chrissie. "Look-a-here. You skirt around this and head for town. Bring that state officer back. Get a posse with him if you can."

"No! What if he recognizes you?"

"I'll worry about that."

"If he arrests you, it'll be my doing. I can't—"

"I disappear pretty good. Look, we need the law in this now, while it's happening."

"But—"

"No buts, Chrissie. This is our chance to bust this wide open."

"Shawnee—"

"This is on you, girl. You got to do this. Get to moving." He smacked Chrissie's horse on the hindquarters to start it moving.

Chrissie kicked her heels into the animal's flank as it took off. Riding in a wide arc around the confusion caused by the stampede, Chrissie rode hard for Fort Worth.

Shawnee made sure she was clear and on her way, then he urged Gray forward to seek Cletus out and rejoin the fight.

16

SHAWNEE AND CLETUS WATCHED AS the few hundred yards between the two forces closed quickly. Now in full flight mode fueled by the gunfire behind them, the cattle ran headlong to escape it, threatening anything in their path. Bynum and his men had no choice but to break ranks and scatter for safety.

Veering to his right, Cletus sighted on Bynum making for a boulder outcropping within reach as the herd barreled through the center of the raiders' abandoned position. Shawnee spotted Rawls and Kaylo going to their left, narrowly missed by the onslaught of the frenzied cattle. Each of the other outlaws found his own route of escape as they fled in every direction available.

Cletus and Shawnee pulled up short.

Cletus scowled. "I want Bynum."

Shawnee pointed at Rawls and Kaylo. "Then I'll get those. Watch yourself, pard."

Each broke into an immediate gallop, chasing his chosen target.

AS CLETUS CUT CROSS-COUNTRY toward the rocks that would afford Bynum cover, he saw the herd completely displace the rest of the raiders. While Terry and a few cowhands continued after the cattle to round them up and contain them, the majority of the Tell riders pursued the fleeing gunmen. Cletus reckoned his boys were pissed off, had had enough, and wanted to end this. He was at full gallop as he watched Bynum round a bend and disappear from his view.

Pulling up sharply just before the turn, Cletus dropped from the saddle and moved ahead on foot. Bynum might have set a trap, maybe an ambush. Cletus looked to present as small a target as possible. Hugging the boulder, he rounded it to see Bynum climbing for all he was worth up the rock face. He aimed a shot after Bynum that only took a chunk out of a rock. Shit! His accuracy was never that good, even up close. At this distance, his gun was next to useless.

Cletus holstered the piece and raced to the spot where Bynum had started his climb. He started up, taking care to place his steps on the flattest surfaces he could find. Casting an eye skyward from time to time, he kept Bynum in view. Halfway up, he saw Bynum reach the top and scramble over a ledge onto what looked to be level ground. Now Bynum was in a position where he could get a shot off without exposing himself. Cletus kept climbing, gambling that Bynum was more interested in escaping than fighting.

Following the natural path eons had carved into the stone, Cletus balanced speed with care as he ascended. He was determined to nail that son-of-a-bitch once and for all but not at the cost of his own life.

As Cletus approached the point at which he could pull himself onto a flat surface, he saw Bynum lean over the edge, his gun aimed downward. Bynum fired one shot as Cletus hugged the rock face to avoid impact. The slug pinged off the stone inches from Cletus's face, spraying him with fragments that bit at his skin. Intending to fight back, Cletus reached for his revolver. Bynum's next attempt found the hammer of his revolver falling on an empty chamber. He pulled himself back from the edge. Cletus left his gun holstered and renewed his climb, attempting to reach Bynum before the man could reload.

At just below the ledge, Cletus pushed his hat off and inched up so only the top of his head and his eyes were above the surface. Bynum was in a crouched position a few yards away, loading his weapon. Cletus thanked his lucky stars that cap and ball pistols did not load as quick as cartridge firing rifles. He pushed himself onto the surface and rolled away from the edge before getting up.

Bynum spotted Cletus. He straightened up and stopped what he was doing. Cletus moved forward, never taking his eyes off Bynum, as Bynum's arms went out to his sides, his right hand clutching the empty revolver. He stood his ground.

Cletus advanced faster without touching his weapon. He preferred fists to guns anyway and would willingly wail the be-jeezus out of this bastard. His expression told Bynum as much as he closed in.

Then, with a sudden move, Bynum let out a growl and threw the empty revolver at Cletus.

Cletus gauged this a last ditch effort as he ducked the weapon's path. It clattered on the stone behind him. Two more long strides put him within striking distance of Bynum. He landed a left jab on Bynum's nose that shot the man's head back and shoved him another foot back. As Bynum recovered, Cletus stepped in and swung a wide right cross that hit the other man on the point of his chin, ripping his head to the side. Momentum carried his body in the same direction. He bounded into the boulder behind him, smashing against it with a grunt.

Cletus stopped, taking in an aggressive stance, silently telling Bynum this was not over. Not hardly.

Blood drooled from Bynum's nose into his open mouth. He spat it out. A jagged cut on his chin oozed blood. He pushed himself away from the stone, moving back into the fight, but Cletus noted the blows he had landed had slowed Bynum, causing him to move erratically.

Bynum raised his right hand in an attempt at a chop to Cletus's head. Cletus easily threw up his left arm to block the punch and slammed his right fist squarely into Bynum's stomach, doubling him over. Now enjoying this, Cletus clasped his hands together and raised them over his head, bringing them down in a blow to the back of Bynum's neck. Bynum grunted from the impact and dropped to his hands and knees, injured and breathless.

Cletus stepped back and again waited, breathing hard. "Come on, big man. Get you up." He danced in place a bit, like the bare-knuckle prizefighter he'd once been. And it came back to him, that life of a slave he'd put behind him, thanks to Mr. Tell. That fighter's death came back to him as well. It didn't matter that it was an accident, he should have pulled that punch. No reason that man had to die.

But this one, this here son of a bitch, different breed of cat altogether. Him, I ain't holding back on. He don't make it, it couldn't happen to anyone more deserving.

Bynum sucked in deep breaths and shook his head to clear it. As Cletus moved closer, Bynum pushed forward, slamming his shoulder into Cletus's legs. The unexpected impact upset Cletus's balance. He fell to the side and landed hard on his shoulder and hip. Bruised and momentarily stunned, Cletus rolled onto his back as Bynum stood up and moved in.

Bynum reached down to grip Cletus, grabbing a handful of his jacket. As his head cleared, Cletus got his feet under him and pushed up. He collided with Bynum's arms and shoved hard, pushing Bynum's arms up, breaking his grip.

Momentum carried Bynum backward. He used his arms and legs to steady himself, leaving himself unguarded. Cletus ducked low and stepped in. He landed two body blows that doubled Bynum over. Then he followed them with an uppercut that connected hard with Bynum's nose. It straightened Bynum and caused more injury and bleeding, but it did not put him down.

Cletus shook pain from his fist, then took another step forward and threw more body punches to sapped Bynum's wind. He swore he felt ribs break upon landing the last blow. Pulling the man around with his back to the edge of a precipice, he slammed a combination left jab and right cross to Bynum's head. He felt the sting of the last punch shoot up his arm as Bynum bounded back close to the overhang. Still on his feet but laboring to stay in the fight, Bynum numbly tried to swing a wide blow. Cletus ducked it and threw another stomach punch and an uppercut. Bynum straightened up and bounded back further, now appearing completely out of it.

Cletus shook his hand hard to restore sensation back into it as he watched Bynum's body pitch backward and fall helplessly over the cliff. Cletus took quick steps to the edge to see Bynum in the midst of rolling down a slope that had to be forty feet long. After several seconds, Bynum reached level ground, rolling a time or two more before stopping and sprawling out. Cletus stared down a moment more to determine movement, but Bynum remained motionless.

Now working on regaining his wind, Cletus briefly considered trying to get to his opponent but discarded the thought. *That piss ant ain't worth the effort.* Whether Bynum was alive or dead, this was over. It was time he got back to the herd.

After a few more heavy breaths, Cletus turned from the precipice and went back to the more gentle incline he'd used to climb up. Slowly and carefully, he started down.

SHAWNEE RODE GRAY FLAT OUT in pursuit of Rawls and Kaylo as the two outlaws fled toward the boulders on the south side of the skirmish site. Gray's stamina and training worked to steadily close the gap. Noting that their mounts were tiring, Shawnee kept up the pace, forcing them further into an area that became inaccessible to horses. They would be forced to dismount and climb to continue their escape, or they would have to stand and fight. Shawnee spooked them even more by firing a shot after them. He had no thought of hitting either of them but sought to intensify their flight response, to cloud their thinking. It appeared to accomplish the purpose.

They galloped into the boulder-strewn area where Shawnee and Gray had rescued the herd. It was surrounded on three sides with rock face sheer enough to prevent horses from effectively climbing them, forcing the outlaws to stop abruptly. Looking around, they saw Shawnee's rapid approach. They dismounted and separated. Rawls began a straight ascent up the boulders, while Kaylo decided to run to the right, seeking an escape path on level ground.

Shawnee raced in behind the abandoned horses. Kaylo's bull-whip, affixed to his gun belt, was in full view as he ran away. Shawnee made the connection between it and the slash mark he'd found on Gray's side and settled on this man as the perpetrator.

He pulled Gray up and dropped from the saddle, intending to pursue Rawls. Gray made a growling sound that Shawnee took to indicate anger. "He's the one, boy. Go get him."

Seeming to understand the words, Gray nodded and took up pursuing Kaylo.

Shawnee went to the boulders and started up as Rawls, halfway up, climbed with everything he had. Shawnee's ascent was measured and careful. Rawls, on the other hand, slipped and made missteps on his way up, allowing Shawnee to close the gap between them.

Watching Rawls disappear from view over the ridge, and assuming the surface there was much flatter, Shawnee slowed his climb and pulled his revolver. He crept up to the edge for an advance look, using the cover of rocks. His eyes broached the space above the boulder rim. A shot in front of him sent a round pinging off the stone a few inches forward of his face. Instantly, he dropped below the surface.

Shawnee's mistake in not removing his hat had exposed him to unnecessary danger, but it had also caused Rawls to fire a shot. That was one less round Rawls had before going empty. Shawnee would use that to his advantage.

Moving to his left, he pulled himself to a spot where the verge was higher. He removed his hat and pushed up for a look. A two foot section of flat rock in front of him dropped off into a depression about four feet deep. An outcropping of boulder six feet forward of the hollow presented a perfect hiding spot. Shawnee made the assumption that Rawls was concealed somewhere in there. Now he needed to determine the exact position.

He lowered himself below the periphery and reached around without looking. His hand settled on a stone as big as his fist. He heaved it out toward the spot from which he'd first looked over the edge. The rock clattered loudly and elicited another shot from Rawls's gun. Assuming the gun had been full, that left three rounds. Good. He would keep Rawls's attention on that spot.

Shawnee repeated the rock-throwing maneuver, drawing another round. *Down to two and shooting at noises.* This was working. *Funny what scared men will do.* Shawnee pulled himself high enough above the edge to aim a shot at the general area from which he guessed

Rawls had fired. Gunsmoke still lingered in the air, rising over Rawls's hiding spot. A passing breeze swept the smoke away. Shawnee fired and immediately dropped below the surface. He crawled back to his original spot. Rawls fired back, leaving one round in the gun.

Shawnee waited for Rawls to make the next move. Rawls was unnerved, Shawnee was certain of that. That would cause Rawls to make bad decisions. It was just a matter of time, time Shawnee was willing to invest. He peered over the edge.

A tense minute passed. Slowly, Rawls emerged from behind the boulders. He must have gotten curious enough to venture out. Good. Shawnee waited, letting it play out.

Rawls moved in a crouch, trying to minimize his exposure while checking for his opponent's location. When he was in the open and close enough, Shawnee pulled himself up so the upper half of his body was above the rock. He had the man dead on and plenty of time to aim a kill shot. *But, no, the bastard's got more value alive, or alive enough to tell what he knows, to expose whatever this scheme against the Tell is and who's running it.*

Instead of firing, Shawnee called out. "Hey!"

Rawls turned toward the voice.

Shawnee rose up. "Drop it."

Rawls raised his weapon and automatically triggered a round that went wild. At the same time, using skilled aim, Shawnee fired, hitting Rawls's left arm above the elbow. Rawls spun from the impact and dropped to a knee but held onto his gun. Blood from the wound stained his shirt sleeve.

Shawnee climbed onto the rock surface and jumped down the four foot drop, landing solidly on both feet, flexing his knees to break the impact. He approached Rawls slowly, carefully, training his revolver dead on the man. "You're empty. Let the gun go."

Rawls looked dumbly across at Shawnee. There was pain on his face, but there was submission there as well. Balancing himself on his knees, he tossed the empty revolver. It clattered on the stone two feet away.

Shawnee moved in close enough to check on Rawls's wound. Rawls put a hand over the slug's entry. Blood now ran through his fingers and into the sleeve material. Shawnee holstered his gun and pulled the bandana from Rawls's neck. "Take your hand away." When Rawls had complied, Shawnee wrapped the bandana around the arm above the wound and tied it off as a makeshift tourniquet, slowing the blood flow. Rawls winced at the tightness.

Leaning in to examine the lesion more carefully, Shawnee announced his findings. "Went right through. Ain't nothing broke. Hurts like hell, but it'll heal. Could a been a heap worse."

Rawls growled. "Who the hell are you? Some kind of gunfighter?"

"Ain't one you'll want to tangle with again." Shawnee straightened up. "That's all you need to know."

Rawls rested back on his haunches. "You going to let me bleed to death?"

"If'n that was so, I wouldn't a went to the trouble of wrapping you up like I done." Shawnee pointed to the bandana. "Naw, there's talking you need to do, but truth be told, you try anything or hold anything back, I'll drop you and not bat an eye doing it."

Rawls thought for a second. "I don't know nothing about nothing." His tone was belligerent.

"We'll see about that later. Right now, we got a tad of down climbing to do."

Rawls looked up at Shawnee, a frown on his face. "How the hell am I supposed to climb like this?"

Shawnee grinned. "Real careful-like, I'd say. Now get moving."

Rawls grunted as he got to his feet.

"I'll be right beside you." Shawnee slapped his holster. "And mine ain't empty."

Rawls moved to the edge and turned so he faced the slope, then he lowered one leg to a spot on the incline to support himself. He started down slowly and carefully.

Shawnee moved over a few feet and started his own descent. Staying close beside Rawls, Shawnee let him set the pace since he had only one useable arm. Rawls grunted and strained as he used muscles he was not accustomed to engaging. Finally, his foot touched the ground. He let go of his hold on the slope and collapsed there, completely exhausted.

Shawnee jumped the remaining couple feet his climb had left, landing hard. This would prevent any loss of time in which Rawls might try to escape, not that he had the wherewithal to do it. Reaching out, Shawnee grabbed Rawls's shirt and lifted him to shaky limbs.

As they both caught their wind, Gray appeared from behind the boulders and trotted to Shawnee. Shawnee greeted the horse with a pat, but his attention was drawn to Gray's front legs and hooves. Fresh blood covered the hooves and had splattered on the legs, reaching to the knees.

"Got him, huh? Good boy."

Shawnee saw Rawls glancing at the hooves. He knew Rawls had figured it out. A thought occurred to Shawnee. "You was the other one holding them Tell horses, wasn't you?"

Rawls kept his eyes on Gray's hooves. "Well, yeah,"

"All right, then. You tell me what I want to know, or how 'bout I turn Gray here loose on you? He'll take care of you right and proper-like."

Rawls shrank back, picturing Kaylo's encounter with Gray. The move he made tugged at the hold Shawnee had on his shirt. "Hold on. No need for that. I'll talk to you."

Shawnee smiled. "Figured as much. Get mounted."

Turned loose from Shawnee's grip, Rawls moved slowly to his horse and, with difficulty, stepped on. Shawnee got up on Gray. He bared his revolver and waved it at the trail. Rawls touched his heels to his horse's flanks to start it moving. Shawnee followed.

17

LATE IN THE MORNING, WITH the sun reaching toward its noon high, Sergeant Malahide, with Chrissie at his side, led a ten man posse out from Fort Worth toward the site of the attack. With Chrissie out front alongside Malahide, the group rode at a gallop, causing the trip to consume only a quarter hour before they came within view of the aftermath of the incident.

As they approached, Chrissie could see the herd milling about while several Tell hands rode slowly around the perimeter to keep the cattle bunched together and quiet. A short distance behind the herd, Tell riders kept watchful eyes and ready guns on the remainder of the gunmen they had captured.

Malahide led the posse to this area as Terry broke away from his guard duty and rode toward them. Both Terry and the lawmen pulled up a few feet from each other.

Malahide gestured to the scene ahead. "What's all this?"

"They threw down on us. We turned it on 'em and grabbed them that we could."

"Rustlers?"

Terry shook his head. "More'n that. Come at us like they wanted to kill us all. Most of 'em took off south."

Malahide nodded, turning to his posse members. "You men go ahead on and run 'em down." The posse split off and headed in the direction Terry pointed out.

As Malahide rode off toward the scene at the herd, Chrissie joined Terry.

"Where did Cletus and Shawnee go?"

"Both chased after some rannies that was part of the attack." Terry pointed. "Ain't seen Shawnee yet, but that surely looks to be Cletus yonder."

Craning her neck to look in that direction, Chrissie saw Cletus coming toward them at a gallop. They dismounted and waited as Cletus closed the distance and pulled up next to them, his black skin glistening with perspiration.

He dismounted wearily. "See you brung the law."

"Shawnee sent me for them. Are you all right?"

"Banged up a tad, but otherwise, I just dandy." Cletus smiled.

As they spoke, Malahide returned to them. "From what I heard from your cowboys, I got enough to hold 'em for trial. Any idea what this was all about or who ran it?"

Cletus spoke up. "I'll tell you what this is about. Somebody be out to run the Tell into the ground. We knows the why, and we knows the who, but we can't prove none of it, so I ain't saying no more. Thought I had somebody I could squeeze it out of—that Bynum ranny. He headed up them *hombres* today, but he had a accident up in the hills. Don't reckon he made it."

"*Cade* Bynum?" Malahide showed interest.

"Yup."

"He dead?"

"Maybe."

"You have something to do with that... accident?"

"Maybe."

"You and him tangled back a ways if memory serves."

Cletus pointed emphatically to the ground beneath him. "It was this here, not that there, what drug me after him. All I'm saying on that as well."

Malahide chewed on that for a bit. "Well... all right, just see you hang around till I'm done checking this whole thing out."

Cletus nodded. "I'll be around."

"Hey." Terry looked beyond the herd. "There be Shawnee. And he's got company."

Shawnee rode at a slow pace behind Rawls as they cut their way through the cattle. His gun could be seen covering Rawls. They reined in nearby.

"Get down," Shawnee told Rawls.

Both men dismounted. Shawnee shoved Rawls closer to the small group.

"He's the one that hid our horses." Chrissie indicated Rawls.

"One of 'em. He'll be talking up 'bout that and more he knows what's good for him." The barrel of Shawnee's gun poked Rawls in the back. "Ain't that so, friend?"

Rawls nodded silently.

Chrissie glanced at Malahide to see him studying Shawnee intently. He moved closer to the two men, lifting his revolver from its holster as he went. He held the gun along his leg pointed at the ground. Taking another step nearer to Shawnee, he tried to raise the gun.

Shawnee moved his gun in line with Malahide's chest. "Drop it." Malahide froze with his revolver halfway to level. "Next time, don't telegraph. I said drop it."

"Shawnee, no," Chrissie shouted. Her words had no effect as Shawnee stood his ground.

Malahide appeared to consider both possibilities, either shoot faster or take a bullet. After a second, he let the iron fall.

"That's better. Figured it was just a matter of time 'fore you worked it out. Most do after a spell."

"Yeah. Alonzo Pearce, wanted dead or alive. You won't get far. I'll track you down, whatever it takes."

"'Fraid that's been tried a time or two. Ain't worked yet. Now, here's what's going to happen. This one and me, we're riding out of here." Shawnee stepped behind Rawls and grabbed his shirt. He backed up, pulling Rawls with him to where Gray stood with Rawls's horse. "You try following, that's a mistake you won't make twice." That was directed at Malahide.

Chrissie took a step forward. "Shawnee, please, think about what you're doing."

"Nothing to think on, Chrissie. Way it's got to be." Shawnee pushed Rawls closer to his horse. "Get up there."

Rawls obeyed, mounting painfully.

Shawnee crossed in front of Gray and backed up to the saddle. He switched his gun to his left hand. Gripping the saddle horn with his right hand, he hopped up, his left foot catching the stirrup. With one smooth move he stepped up and swung his right leg across Gray's neck. Never taking his eyes off Malahide, Shawnee seated himself in the saddle. He called to Rawls. "Move out. Back the way we come."

Rawls pulled his horse around and started out toward the cattle. Shawnee fell in behind. They were galloping by the time they reached the herd. The cattle separated as they rode through.

Instantly, Malahide stooped and picked up his revolver. He raised it and trained it on Shawnee, but Chrissie stepped in front of him, blocking the shot.

"No, please, don't." She raised her hands in front of him.

Malahide made a discontented face. "Well, no, reckon I can't. Not now."

Shawnee and Rawls kept going, creating distance and riding out of pistol range.

Angry and frustrated, Malahide shoved his gun back in its holster. "Young lady, you just interfered with—"

"There's a lot you don't know. Please... just let him go."

Malahide huffed. "Got no choice now, but let me tell you, you ever pull something like that there again, I'll put you behind bars, woman or no, faster'n you can say Jack Robinson." He stomped angrily back to his horse and mounted.

Cletus stepped close to Chrissie and whispered to her, "Your pa'd be right proud of you about now." He mounted and joined Malahide. "I'll side you."

Malahide scowled. "I don't need your help."

"I got my own reasons." Cletus looked over his shoulder. "Chrissie, you mind taking the herd on? I'll wait for you in town."

She nodded.

Pulling his horse around sharply, Malahide headed quickly back to where the raiders were being held. Cletus followed.

Chrissie watched as Shawnee and Rawls became mere specks on the horizon. She forced her mind back to the task at hand. "Come on, Terry, let's get to that trail herd before they leave."

"Yes, ma'am, we'll get 'er done."

BY A LITTLE PAST NOON, with not a cloud in the sky, the sun had gone from warm to hot, even in the cooler month of March. In the chasm that became the landing spot for Cade Bynum's body after it rolled down the steep slope hours earlier, the stone reflected heat from the sunlight. With the inability of the wind to reach the location because of the high rock walls around the gorge, very little air circulated around Bynum as he lay face down, motionless in a twisted posture.

He stirred, just a twitch at first. Sense returned slowly but steadily, causing erratic, jerky movements. Over the span of a few minutes, coming back to consciousness, he straightened his body and rolled onto his side, all the while groaning and screaming in pain. His eyes fluttered, then opened to hazy, distorted images of the rock slope he faced. Blinking cleared away some of the blurring as memory of the fight and fall crept into his mind. Combined with the dizziness, everything seemed distant and upended, random snippets of what had happened earlier.

He tried sitting up, but when his left arm touched the ground, he cried out in pain. This agony was so intense that it instantly snapped him back to full perception. Glancing down at the arm, its contorted shape told him it was likely broken below the elbow. Overwhelmed, he collapsed onto his back, the arm splayed out to his side. He lay there as countless minutes passed.

The sun above blazed into his eyes, narrowing his vision. Shutting his eyes worked only momentarily. The brightness shown red through his closed eyelids to the point of causing him to turn his head away. His body felt as if it was baking. Perspiration rolled off his skin and joined the already present bloodstains on his shirt. Beads of sweat streamed off his face onto the stone on which he lay. He had to get out of there before he fried.

Bynum shook his head to clear it. That only served to make the vertigo he experienced worse. His left arm was useless, he knew that now. Sitting up would only make his head spin more. He knew that as well, but he had to do something to get clear of this oven he was in before it sapped what little strength he had left. Using his right arm, he forced himself up. The first attempt failed. His head swirled almost into oblivion. He dropped on his back, exhausted, and remained there to catch his breath and regain some semblance of power and control.

Moments went by. Normal breathing returned. His head began to clear. There was no renewed strength, but he knew he had to move, even if it made his injuries worse. He rolled to his side and slowly, using his right hand to stabilize himself, pushed up to a sitting position. He had to stop there.

More time passed. Bynum's mind and body acclimated to that posture. He rolled to his knees, supporting himself with his right hand. His left arm hung down, useless. Additional pain emitted from the bone break, but he endured it. This cost more time while he adjusted to it.

Untold minutes passed. He finally felt up to taking the next step. He pulled his right leg up so his foot was flat on the ground. Then he raised to a position on one knee and straightened up. From there, he pushed his right arm against the knee and forced himself to stand. Wobbly at first, but determined, he steadied himself and took a step, more like a stagger. Drunk without the fun of drinking.

A few more steps brought him to the rock wall in front of him. He reached out and leaned against the stone for support. Out of direct sunlight, it felt cooler to the touch. He looked around slowly, trying to orient himself. Given that he had fallen down the side of the boulder he'd climbed to, he gauged that his horse should be ahead and around to the right, assuming the animal hadn't wandered off. Getting to the horse became his next task. He supported himself on the stone wall as he moved forward.

Several yards into the journey, the pain from his arm as it dangled uncontrollably became distracting and almost overwhelming. There had to be a way to ease the thing. After a moment's thought, Bynum's mind worked it out. He stopped and unbuttoned his shirt at the solar plexus. Then, carefully lifting the wounded limb with his right hand and cradling it with his good arm, he guided it through the opening in the shirt to the elbow. This caused additional pain, but the intensity was not as great. He allowed the arm to rest in that crude sling while he moved on. With the limb almost immobile, the pain was lessened.

Making his way around the base of the rock outcropping took longer and was more grueling than he expected, but he powered through it. He stumbled around the last turn to see his horse grazing contentedly exactly where he'd left it. At least something went right.

He leaned away from the wall to test his stability. Still unsteady, but able to stand on his own, he took an unsupported step, then another. Some side-stepping and more stumbling occurred, but he managed to reach the horse. Leaning against the saddle for a few seconds allowed him to collect himself. Then he pulled the reins over the animal's head and placed his foot in the stirrup. After a second to gather strength, he hauled himself up into the saddle and took a second to process the associated pain before he started the horse at a slow walk.

Once he recognized the country he was in and became reoriented, Bynum directed his mount toward Fort Worth. He now had a simple plan. He would see the doc to get his arm fixed up, then seek out Manion, who had hired him in the first place, and collect what was coming to him. Cutting his losses was in order. He'd crossed the line. The nigga'd seen his face, knew he was part of this hair-brained scheme, and by now likely had the ear of that lawman. Going back to Fort Worth was chancy, but he needed medical attention and money. Fort Worth had both. But as far as anybody knew, the fall had killed him, so getting in and out of Fort Worth would be easier. Then he'd leave for parts unknown to keep it that way.

18

THE MID-AFTERNOON SUN BURNED brightly over Fort Worth. It had warmed to the point that coats were not needed, but as Bynum entered the town, he felt cold. Worn out and hungry to the point of distraction, it would have taken a fire built directly under him to dispel the shivers he experienced. Pain prevented him from moving any faster. He walked his horse to the rear of the doctor's office and stopped. After a long moment to recoup, he swung wearily down from the saddle and had to hang onto the thing to keep from falling while he recovered from that effort. He rested his head against the leather and took another minute to gather strength.

After a few cleansing breaths, he made his way through the alley to the front of the office. As he stepped inside, he ran a few scenarios through his clouded mind to answer the questions he was sure the doc would ask.

Doctor Ramsey looked up from his desk. "May I—oh, bollocks, you've had a time, haven't you?"

Bynum moved forward. "Had a mite of a fall-down, Doc. Need some fixing." He sat heavily in the chair in front of the desk.

Ramsey stood and rounded the desk. "No doubt. Come here. Let's have a look."

For the next hour, Ramsey worked on his patient, setting the break, placing the arm in a cast and sling, and cleaning and treating various cuts and bruises. Much to Bynum's surprise, the doctor asked no questions. Bynum chalked that up to him being a frontier doctor and dealing with all manner of folks. Bynum kept his mouth shut.

After paying the fee, Bynum left and returned to his horse. He picked up the reins and led the animal across the street, into an alley, and walked past the few buildings separating him from the rear of the bank. There he stopped and dropped the reins. He reached into his saddle bag and fished out a spare revolver, a short barrel Colt's Pocket Police model. Dropping it into his empty holster, he moved unsteadily to the door. He pounded it continually until Manion opened it.

Standing in the doorway, Manion was aghast. "Bynum! What the hell—"

Bynum pushed past him. "Shut up. Let me by."

Bynum limped slowly to the guest chair and sat down heavily, Manion turned in disbelief and shut the door.

"I take it the raid went badly."

Bynum looked up. "Yeah, something like that. Ever get near run down by a stampede, then shoved off of a cliff?"

Manion shook his head. "Can't say I have."

"Well, I can." Bynum drew in a long breath and exhaled loudly. "And you know what, I'm done with this shit. Pay me off right now, and I be gone quick as a wink. That nigga thinks me dead. I'm keeping it that way."

Manion's breath quickened. "No, you can't do that. We need you."

Bynum pulled out his revolver. "I don't give a shit what you need. I'm taking care of me. So, you get me my cash money... now."

Manion hesitated. "I—"

"Now! I look like I'm joking or something?"

"N-no."

"Then get the goddamn money."

Manion raised both hands in a calming gesture. "All right, all right, calm down. I'll get it." He rounded the desk and kneeled down at a small metal safe standing against the wall. Nervous fingers needed two tries to dial the correct combination, but he managed to get the door open.

Bynum heard the noise. "Don't bother counting it. I'll take whatever's there."

Again, Manion hesitated.

"Come on, make it fast. Or maybe I should just put a slug in your gizzard and take it myself."

Manion rose with the money in hand. "Hold on." He shook a finger in the air. "You might be right about leaving."

Bynum shot him a confused look. "Come again?"

"I've had my doubts about this thing from the beginning. At every turn, my nerves have become more frazzled. Bremmer's becoming more and more reckless. I'm afraid he's going to put us all in jeopardy."

"What the hell're you blabbing about?"

"I think we should both just go, split what's here down the middle and just go. Leave Bremmer to fend for himself."

Bynum caught up and caught on. Then his mind worked. "I don't give a shit about him. And I don't give a shit about you going or staying. But I ain't splitting nothing with you. What you got there is mine. I earned it and then some. I'm taking it now. You get your own."

IN THE ALLEY LEADING TO the rear of the bank, Bremmer

stopped short as he rounded the corner. The sight of Bynum's horse standing idly near the door made him suspicious. He questioned why Bynum would be here instead of with the raiders. Proceeding to the door, he stopped first to listen before entering. The voices inside were muffled, but he could make out that they were Manion and Bynum. While he could not make out all the words, the references to splitting and leaving were clear. *Oh, no, not now. Not when we're this close.* He pulled out a small Derringer two-shot pistol from his jacket and held it ready as he turned the doorknob to find it unlocked. The door opened quietly, allowing him to step in without immediate notice.

"Bynum!" Bremmer raised the small piece. "I've got you in my sights. Don't move."

Bynum froze and said nothing.

Manion, still clutching the money, let out a breath. "Jarrett, you're just in time. He was going to kill me."

Bremmer moved closer. He pulled the gun out of Bynum's hand and stepped back, retaining the use of his own weapon. "What's this about leaving?" His first full sight of Bynum's face and body prompted a change of query. "What the hell happened to you?"

"Them Tell riders fought back. Stampeded the cattle right at us so's we had to scatter every which way. Then that nigga chases me down and heaves me off a cliff."

"So you failed."

Bynum's brow furrowed. "That's what you're worried about? Shit, I'm lucky I'm still alive."

Manion broke in. "That's not all, Jarrett. He wants to run out on us. Wanted me to pay him off."

"And, of course, you were going to?"

"He… he had that gun on me. I had no choice."

Bremmer shot him a foul look. "Shut up! I heard enough before

I came in. That told me everything I need to know. You pathetic morons. All the planning, all the work, to come down to this?" He looked off into space, considering his next move. He had to change plans to control this before it got out of hand. The new plan called for drastic action. "No, I can't have this. None of it. There's too much riding on it."

With a sudden move, Bremmer raised his Derringer and fired point blank at Bynum. At such close range, the slug doubled Bynum over as it cut into his chest. He slumped forward and dropped to the floor, curled up in a ball.

Manion panicked. "Jarrett, my god, what are you doing? You'll have the whole town in here."

Bremmer turned to face Manion. "Let 'em come. You idiots killed each other. I was never here."

Manion was aghast as Bremmer turned Bynum's gun on him. He raised his hands in a wretched appeal. "Jarrett, no!" He shrank back with nowhere to run.

"Yes." Bremmer cocked the revolver and fired, catching Manion squarely in the chest. The impact slammed him against the wall. He sank to a heap on the floor as the money fluttered in all directions.

Quickly, Bremmer dropped the revolver near Bynum's body and tossed the Derringer over the desk to land near Manion's remains. He rushed out and slammed and locked the back door as pounding could be heard on the door leading in from the bank. Frantic voices called to Manion. Bremmer moved fast behind the buildings, away from the bank.

Using an alley a block away, Bremmer moved out to the street to fold in with the rush of citizens responding to calls of shots coming from the bank. He went with them, staying in the background as they approached the bank in a disorganized throng. Questions and comments sounded around him, none of which were intelligible. Bremmer went with the flow.

In a few moments, Sergeant Malahide, with Cletus at his side, reined up, dismounted, and pushed into the main body of towns-people. Bremmer kept an eye on Cletus, who stayed on the outskirts of the crowd.

Malahide's authoritative voice quieted the throng. "What's go-ing on here?"

Many answers came at once, making it difficult for anyone to understand. Finally, a bank employee stepped up and gave a concise account of what he'd observed. He'd heard shots and broke into Mr. Manion's office. He'd found Mr. Manion and a stranger dead, both shot. He guessed they shot each other.

Malahide entered the bank. Bremmer, satisfied his makeshift plan had worked, turned and walked away.

———————

WITH RAWLS RIDING WEARILY IN front of him, Shawnee di-rected his captive into the main area of the Tell Ranch. The scene was quiet. All the hands were out with the trail herd or tending the remaining cattle in the field.

As they rode between the ranch house and the bunkhouse, Cook-ie emerged from the cook shack and headed toward the bunkhouse.

Shawnee spotted him. "Cookie."

The cook stopped and looked. He waved recognition of Shaw-nee and waited for them to arrive. "Looks like you been busy."

Shawnee pulled rein and stopped Rawls's horse. "A tad. I need to hide this hombre out a spell. He's got a heap of talking to do. Can you fix up his arm?"

Cookie moved closer and scrunched up his face as he looked over Rawls's wound. "I reckon. You shoot him?"

"Yup."

"Reckon he ain't going to hang around if'n you leave, right?"

"Yup."

"Well, then, we'll tie him to a bunk 'fore I start fixing on him."

Shawnee spoke to Rawls. "You heard the man. Get down."

Rawls obeyed.

Cookie pulled a big Colt Dragoon revolver from his waistband and pointed it at Rawls as Shawnee dismounted. "Don't get any funny idears, either. I be ready, just in case."

Shawnee grinned. "Cookie, I swear, that thing's bigger'n you. Wonder it don't pull down your britches."

Cookie matched his grin. "Shoots a nice big hole though."

Shawnee chuckled, knowing Cookie's words were meant for Rawls. He pointed at the bunkhouse. "Inside."

Reluctantly, Rawls moved toward the building, holding his wounded arm. Shawnee and Cookie followed closely.

Cookie pointed to a nearby bunk. "Stretch you out there."

Rawls painfully did as he was told. Cookie found some lengths of rope and secured Rawls's legs and good arm to the bunk frame. "He ain't going nowheres."

Shawnee nodded. "Fix his arm and hold him here. I'll be back to collect him."

"Sure thing." Cookie chuckled. "'Pears like the Tell's getting nigh onto a hos-a-pital of late."

Shawnee laughed and slapped Cookie playfully on the arm. He hurried outside and stepped up onto Gray. The big horse jumped forward and went into a gallop. Maintaining that speed shortened the length of the trip to Fort Worth by one half. As he came within sight of the town, he slowed Gray and went off the trail to the north. He rode through thick brush until he was again in line with the town. Then he moved slowly to a point just outside the beginning of the buildings and dismounted. He led the horse the rest of the way, coming to the rear of the structures to stay hidden from view.

After examining each place, he located what he believed to be the state police office. He grounded Gray's reins and entered the alley beside it, proceeding to a side window. Muffled voices came through the slightly open sash, voices he identified as belonging to Cletus and the police sergeant. He removed his hat and ventured a glance through the window to orient himself with the layout of the inside. Malahide was at his desk. Cletus stood beside it facing the window.

To get Cletus's attention, Shawnee took the chance of being discovered by Malahide. He placed his face in the window and waved a hand at Cletus. His luck held. Cletus saw him, but Malahide didn't. Shawnee made a gesture toward the rear of the building with his hand. Cletus showed surprise at first, then nodded slightly. Shawnee pulled away from the window and moved back to where Gray stood. He waited.

Cletus rounded the corner from the alley a few seconds later. "Hey, where's that *hombre* you caught? He tell you anything?"

"Rawls? I left him at the Tell. Cookie's got him hogtied. And yeah, he give up that lawyer. He's heading up this whole thing about the Tell. Trying to take it over."

"Then that ties in...." Cletus trailed off, not finishing the statement. He seemed deep in thought.

"What ties in?"

"Reckon that fall back yonder didn't kill Bynum. Somehow, he made it to town and wound up shooting it out with the banker. Can't cipher the why of that, but they both dead, shot each other looks like."

The news started Shawnee thinking. "I don't buy that. That banker fellow, he's too skittish to get caught up in a gunfight. He'd run 'fore he'd fight. More likely that lawyer dropped both of them, figuring they'd turn on him. Where is that son of a bitch, anyways? You seen him?"

"Come to think of it, no, I ain't. Couple a folks said he rode out of town a spell back, really knocking on it."

"Where's Chrissie?"

"Should be on her way back from the trail herd about now."

Then it clicked in Shawnee's mind. "Shit! It does fit. Look, you head out to the ranch and pick up Rawls." There was an immediacy in his words as he went to Gray.

"Where you going?"

Shawnee swung into the saddle. "Chrissie. That bastard's after Chrissie." He pulled Gray around and hurried away, heading east.

19

RIDING AT A FLAT-OUT gallop, Shawnee headed in the general direction of the trail herd, which he knew to be camped east of town. The picture in his head of Bremmer laying for Chrissie, who he guessed would use this main road to get back to Fort Worth, caused him to stay on the trail instead of cutting across country. Having no idea how far ahead the lawyer was, his mission became reaching Chrissie before Bremmer could.

It all fit together now. Shawnee put the whole scheme together in his head as he rode. Bremmer killed Bynum and Manion when they presented a threat to his plans. If they testified against him, Bremmer faced a stiff prison sentence at least. With that danger laid to rest, so to speak, Bremmer would be able to take immediate possession of the Tell once he got rid of the last stumbling block, Chrissie. Eliminating her gave him a clear path to make the bank a meager offer to take the place off their hands. They'd likely jump at the chance to get out from under a failing business. Then Bremmer would be exactly where he wanted to be. Shawnee resolved to prevent Bremmer from taking over the Tell or harming Chrissie, but he had to find Chrissie first.

"Come on, Gray. We got to get to her. We got to find her."

As he came around a bend in the trail, Chrissie, riding at a re-laxed pace, came into his view. At this distance, she was just a rider on a horse, but he was sure it was her. He urged Gray to a higher speed to cover the quarter mile between them more quickly. When she spotted him, she reined in and stopped to wait for him. He kept going, waving a hand to try to get her to move off the road into the bushes that lined it. Unable to be more specific, he realized she could not understand what he meant. She simply stayed there in the middle of the trail, waiting, presenting a perfect target.

Shawnee raced over to her and reined. "Get off the trail. He's coming for you."

Stunned, she only managed an unintelligible sound in response.

"Get to cover." Shawnee grabbed the reins from her hands and led the horse into the brush.

"Shawnee, what are you doing? What's wrong?"

"Bremmer. I think he's out to kill you. I got to get you to town 'fore he finds you. Come on."

He directed Gray deeper into the bushes, heading back toward Fort Worth. Chrissie followed closely. They moved slowly, careful-ly, staying under the cover of trees and brush, the densest Shawnee could locate. He kept a sharp eye out for anything that might mean Bremmer was close. He saw nothing, but he had that gnawing feel-ing the man was not far off.

As they headed toward Fort Worth, he explained what had hap-pened earlier to Manion and Bynum—and his assessment of Brem-mer's revised intentions.

"He kills you, he's got a clear shot at the ranch."

That started her ruminating. "You don't suppose he had anything to do with Pa's death, do you?"

Shawnee shook his head. "Naw! He's playing a long game. All he had to do was wait."

Gray broke new trail through the thick underbrush. Well into the journey, the horse pulled up short, whinnying and snorting.

Reading the horse's message, Shawnee drew his sidearm. "We got company."

Chrissie stopped while he scrutinized the area carefully, certain the threat Gray signaled was close enough to be a danger. As he scanned a ridge to their left, the waning sunlight reflected off something metallic. He'd seen something like that before in other situations. It blinded him for a split second, but its source was clear. That was a gun barrel, and it likely belonged to Bremmer.

The shot that followed graphically answered any question he had. A slug slammed into a tree trunk only inches from the pair. Reaching their ears a split second later, the sound of the shot clearly identified the weapon as a rifle.

"Get down!"

Chrissie reacted instantly, dismounting and hunkering down while holding her horse's reins to keep it from bolting. Shawnee followed suit, dropping to a crouch as he scanned the area up to the top of the slope.

A puff of black powder smoke rose lazily from the shooter's position several yards below the ridgeline and dissipated in the breeze.

Shawnee holstered his six-shooter. Useless at this range. Scurrying around Gray, he pulled the Henry from its saddle scabbard, levering a round into the chamber. He took a kneeling position. "Stay down." Shouldering the rifle, he fired at the general spot from which the gun smoke had ascended, trying to elicit another shot to pinpoint the attacker's location.

It came almost immediately, chipping off a nearby branch.

Shawnee fired into the spot. No return fire came.

Getting Chrissie to safety became the primary mission. If she got far enough away, Shawnee could stalk the shooter without concern for her.

"Chrissie." He kept his eyes on the ridge. "You do exactly like I tell you, hear?"

"Yes." Her answer told him she might actually listen this time.

He waited, sighting across the barrel of the Henry at the mild slope. Tense seconds passed. Another shot from a slightly different location went wild, but it signaled that their assailant was now closer. Shawnee pumped a round in response toward the new position, marked by the gun smoke rising above it. This drew another shot. It also hit nothing.

"When I tell you,"—Shawnee scanned the ridge—"mount up and hightail it for town. I'll cover you. Bring that sergeant back with you. You savvy?"

"Yes."

Shawnee fired three rounds in rapid succession. "Go." He continued firing, getting off another three rounds.

Chrissie swung into the saddle and slammed her heels into the horse's flanks, staying low. The horse took off as fast as the thicket would allow, taking her from the scene. When he was sure she was clear, Shawnee held his fire.

He waited for Bremmer's next move.

Nothing came.

Time to take the fight to Bremmer.

Crouching, Shawnee moved forward, staying to the dense brush for concealment. He expected Bremmer to be on the move as well, trying for a better, closer position.

Shawnee continued to climb the slope, heading directly for the last spot Bremmer had occupied. As he closed the distance, he realized the ridgeline was also the road between Fort Worth and the trail herd, the same trail Chrissie had been traveling. That being true, Bremmer's horse would have to be tied off somewhere nearby. It made sense to locate the animal and keep Bremmer separated from it to limit his options. Further, Shawnee reasoned that if Bremmer came from Fort Worth, the horse would be tethered west of Bremmer's location. Shawnee changed direction slightly to reach the top of the ridge slightly west of where Bremmer ambushed them. Once he located the horse, he planned to release it, scare it off, and then continue to move east in search of Bremmer.

It was quiet when Shawnee crested the hill. No shots had been fired since his last round. He crouched upon reaching level ground and scanned the area. A dense pine forest across the narrow dirt road offered the best concealment. He got up and, carrying the rifle at port arms, hurried across the trail and went into the woods deep enough to stay out of sight. Moving forward then, he stayed within the tree line but close enough to the road to see any activity clearly.

After moving east one hundred yards, he came within sight of a tethered saddle horse. It was tied by its reins to a branch on the side of the trail just outside the tree line. Shawnee made the assumption that this was Bremmer's mount. He approached carefully, as silently as possible. The horse was busy grazing and did not react as Shawnee reached it. He untied the reins and dropped them. Stepping back, he waved his hands and the rifle frantically and shouted at the horse in a coarse whisper. "Hyaah! Get out of here!" The horse shied and backed away. Shawnee took a step forward and continued his gyrations until the animal turned and took off up the road, going west.

Satisfied that he was now between Bremmer and the horse, Shawnee ducked back into the trees and continued scanning the trail as he moved forward. He had seven rounds left in the rifle and five in the pistol. A quick feel around his cartridge belt counted ten rifle rounds available. He ciphered that should take care of any fight Bremmer might make.

As he moved through the forest, Shawnee caught sight of movement across the trail. He stopped. A figure climbed onto the road from the slope and brushed dust and debris from his rumpled business suit. The man carried a rifle that looked to be a Winchester Yellow Boy. A closer look told Shawnee this was Bremmer, looking more harried than the last time he'd seen him. Bremmer moved in a hunched-over posture toward the woods.

Shawnee shouldered the already cocked Henry as Bremmer reached the middle of the trail. "Stop right there, Bremmer."

Bremmer stopped, hesitated, then darted into the trees. Shawnee fired as Bremmer moved, narrowly missing him. He started forward, levering the rifle. Bremmer disappeared into the forest.

Scouring the trees as he advanced, Shawnee watched for any movement. He counted on the fact that he was more experienced at cat-and-mouse games than his adversary.

A figure scurried noisily from a tree trunk a few yards ahead to another tree farther on. Shawnee kept going, using bushes and pine trees as stopping points to continue his scan. Another movement came, this time slower and louder. Shawnee noted Bremmer was likely tiring. He fired a shot that slammed into the tree as Bremmer darted behind it. Shawnee took cover behind a tree, ready to fire. There was a momentary silence.

"I've got money," Bremmer shouted. His voice was rough, breathless. There was fear in it as well. "I can pay well if you let me go."

As part of the game, Shawnee did bother to reply.

More silence passed.

"What do you say, kid? I can pay." Bremmer's voice sounded more frightened.

Shawnee held his tongue. He'd let him sweat some more.

A few minutes went by.

"Listen." There was bargaining, pleading in Bremmer's speech. "I've got the money on me. I'll leave it right here for you. Right here. Just let me go, let me leave. Please."

Still, Shawnee said nothing. He waited.

"Look. It's right here on the ground. Let me walk away, and it's all yours. Five hundred dollars. Right here." Bremmer's voice was hoarse and shaky now.

That told Shawnee it was time. "Not a chance, you son of a bitch. You'll try to kill me like you tried to kill Chrissie."

"No, you've got it all wrong. I just want to get clear of this."

"Too late for that, partner. I got you dead to rights. You ain't going nowheres."

Now there was silence from Bremmer's location.

Shawnee stepped into the open. It was time to end this. He levered the long gun loudly, shouldered it, and started a slow walk forward, focusing on Bremmer's hiding spot.

With a sudden move, likely from fear turning to panic, Bremmer stepped out beside the tree and brought his rifle up to fire, using the trunk as support. Shawnee, already sighted in, fired one round, hitting the tree inches from Bremmer's face and spraying splinters of bark near his eyes. Bremmer ducked behind the tree.

Shawnee advanced faster, then stopped abruptly within a few yards of Bremmer's concealment. He put three rapid shots into the tree, meant to add to Bremmer's terror. Then he waited.

In a second, Bremmer stepped out from behind the tree, clear of it by a few inches, and returned fire. Both shots went wild. Shawnee levered and fired once, counting that off as his last rifle round. Bremmer folded and staggered back about a foot but remained standing. A blood stain appeared on his jacket at the left shoulder. He stood there for a second as Shawnee moved on him. Bremmer turned and went into a tottering run out of the woods and onto the trail. Shawnee followed.

Bremmer stopped in the middle of the road and looked around as Shawnee cleared the tree line.

"Ain't no cover out here." Shawnee stopped. "No place to run."

Bremmer turned unsteadily to face Shawnee. He labored at working the rifle lever while Shawnee stood his ground. Finally, Bremmer got a round chambered. His wound prevented him from shouldering the gun, so he fired from the hip. The shot went hopelessly astray.

Shawnee shifted his empty rifle to his left hand and drew his side arm as Bremmer fumbled to crank another round in place. Shawnee raised the revolver to eye level and cocked it. Bremmer's mishandling caused his rifle to jam the next round, stopping the lever at half closed. He abandoned his effort and looked up at the hand gun staring him in the face. His eyes darted back and forth as his expression betrayed his panic.

Bremmer sucked in a breath. His voice was shaky, fearful. "If you kill me, you're putting a noose around your black friend's neck,"

Shawnee stopped, maintaining his bead on Bremmer. "What'd you say?"

"Think about it. That police sergeant is no fool. It won't take him long to find out the nigga and I had words. Who do you think he's going to suspect as my killer? Who's he going to look to arrest?"

Shawnee pondered that.

Bremmer continued his argument, his voice calming a little. "If you let me go, let me walk away, your friend is in the clear. And I'll just go. I've had enough. I know I can't win at this. I'll leave the territory. You'll never hear from me again—none of you will ever hear from me again."

Shawnee stared at Bremmer for a long moment, the wheels in his head turning at breakneck speed to square this without endangering Cletus. He looked down at the rifle in his left hand, turning it to see the name carved into the stock. Lon Pearce, it read. He settled on his answer as he returned his gaze to the sights on his weapon.

Without further word, he pulled the trigger, putting a ball into Bremmer's head just above the right eye. Bremmer's head snapped back sharply, beginning a backward trajectory. Then his body folded and sank to the dirt. It twitched uncontrollably for a few seconds, then it was still.

Shawnee advanced slowly, warily, a natural reaction after a shooting. He expected the man to be dead, but that was never certain until verified. Reaching the body, he holstered his revolver and took a knee to feel for a pulse. Nothing.

Kneeling there, Shawnee stared off down the trail as his mind went through a quick recap. Bremmer was dead. His partners were dead. Rawls would tell his story to bargain for less jail time, and that would bring everything out into the open. Chrissie was out of danger and would have her chance to save the Tell. Only one loose end was left hanging, Sergeant Malahide. Chrissie was fetching him here right now. Bremmer was right. Malahide's investigation into Bremmer's death would likely turn up the run-in Cletus had with Bremmer. That would bring him to suspect Cletus of the killing. Having sent Cletus to round up Rawls from the Tell, Shawnee figured Cletus would not be able to account for his time when Bremmer died. He would not have a viable alibi. And even if Shawnee had this blown way out of proportion, and Cletus was not charged, it would still put Cletus through a hell he didn't deserve. Not a possibility Shawnee wanted to leave to chance.

He gazed down at the stock of the Henry. What better proof was there? The body would be found right where it dropped. The Henry would be found beside it, empty, name side up, pegging Lon Pearce as the killer, no question.

He lifted the rifle for a last look. It had been his for four years, ever since he had the run-in with that gambler, Ostro. That shootout gained him a lot. Besides being the incident that made him a killer, it was how he got Gray, Ostro's horse at the time. In the saddle holster he found the Henry and, after a time, like Toby Joe Hawks did with his shotgun, Shawnee carved his name in the stock. He'd had no good reason for doing that, and he never thought then it'd come in handy for something like this, but there you go, made to order. Proof Cletus didn't kill Bremmer.

Shawnee, already wanted for more offenses than he could count, placed the rifle in the position he had chosen and rose from the body. What did it matter that he'd be tagged for this? Added to the other charges against him, it would get lost in the shuffle. It was the least he could do to ensure Cletus would be in the clear and Chrissie would not lose her cherished guardian.

He turned from the scene and went to the ridgeline. With one look back at what he had just done, he started down the slope on an angle that would lead him to the spot where Gray waited.

Picking his way through the rocks and bushes, he reached the horse to find it grazing. Picking up the reins, he stepped up into the saddle. "Guess it's time to move on, boy. We ain't needed here no more." He gently nudged his spurs into Gray's flanks, setting the horse in motion.

20

AS THEY RODE INTO A bend that began the slope line on which Bremmer had attacked Chrissie and Shawnee, Malahide rode slightly ahead of her. She called out, "Hold up!" Her shout caused Malahide to pull a hasty rein as Chrissie stopped in the middle of the road.

"It was right around here. A little further up the trail."

Malahide, still a few paces ahead of her, turned in his saddle to face her. "All right, this is as far as you go. I'll handle it from here. You head back."

"But I can show—"

"I said I'd handle it alone, and that's the all of it. Now you turn around and head on back, you hear?"

Chrissie thought for a second and then nodded. "All right." She turned her horse and set out for Fort Worth at a slower pace.

Malahide faced east and continued up the trail slowly. As he rode, he lifted the revolver in his holster and dropped it back in. Just a precaution to make sure it would come out smoothly if he needed it in a hurry.

The bend softened and then straightened. About two hundred yards ahead, a saddle horse grazed on the side of the road. Malahide approached slowly and took the horse's reins in hand. He continued on, leading the horse behind him.

Moving on another several hundred yards, he came upon a form in the roadbed. It looked like a body, a man's body. Too far to be sure. He kept riding, a little faster now.

Another minute passed, bringing him closer to the object. Definitely a man's body. He pulled up and dismounted, warily scanning the area for threats. Satisfied none were obvious, he moved forward, mentally identifying the corpse as the lawyer, Bremmer. He went to a knee at the body. Immediate repulsion came over him as he viewed the mangled face where the ball had penetrated. There was blood all over, on the clothing, on the ground. It emanated from both the head wound and the one in the shoulder. He lifted a bloody hand and checked for life. No pulse. The limb was still warm, indicating it happened only a short time before. No drag marks were present. It happened right here. He went through the clothes and found Bremmer's wallet in the inside jacket pocket. It contained definite identification. He wondered if this was connected with the Tell girl's ambush story. Did he try to kill her? If so, why?

Malahide rose with a grunt and exhaled heavily. The tunnel vision that had engulfed him upon sighting the body began to abate. He looked around. The weapons came into view. A blood-covered Winchester Yellow Boy with the lever half closed lay on Bremmer's left side near his hand. A Henry with a name carved into the stock was on the body's right. *Lon Pearce*, it said.

Right, Alonzo Pearce, the name on the wanted poster with the likeness of that stranger that showed up at the Tell a spell back. Alonzo Pearce, wanted for everything from petty theft to murder in at least two states. Looked like he had his killer. A couple of questions arose. Was Pearce justified in killing Bremmer? And why did he leave the rifle behind? It was a fool thing to do, identifying himself as the killer. Was he covering for someone else? If so, why? Malahide considered, pondered, but his course was clear. He had his killer. Pearce was a wanted man. He needed to be hunted down and taken, if not for this, then for everything else he was accused of. Nothing left to do now but take the body back to town and start up a manhunt.

Malahide released his camp blanket from the back of his saddle and dropped it near the body. He brought Bremmer's horse closer. Then he rolled the body over, and, with great effort, he bent and lifted the limp form, steadied it, and turned to face the horse. Residual blood dripped onto his clothing. Two effort-filled steps placed him adjacent to the saddle. With a final push, he heaved the body up and onto the saddle, face down. Some adjusting was necessary to balance it in place. He leaned back to catch his breath and replenish lost strength. He was getting too old for shit like this.

Stooping to pick up the blanket, he opened it and draped it across the body. At least women and children in town wouldn't be subjected to the sight of a dead body as he brought it in. Best he could do under these circumstances.

He retrieved the Henry and inserted it in Bremmer's empty saddle holster. That was evidence. With nowhere to store Bremmer's rifle, he decided not to take it. Instead he heaved it over the ridge to land indiscriminately somewhere on the slope. Not as if Bremmer needed it anymore. Then he mounted and gathered up the other horse's reins. He set out slowly for Fort Worth, hoping the jostling wouldn't unseat his cargo.

IT WAS LATE AFTERNOON WHEN Malahide entered Fort Worth. He moved slowly, leading Bremmer's horse behind him. As he moved along the street, bystanders caught sight of the burden the horse carried, and, putting the pieces together, they began collecting around the lawman and following him. He ignored the questions thrown at him from the growing crowd, continuing his ride past his office to the undertaker's location a few doors down.

Drawing rein outside, Malahide dismounted wearily and went inside. The few minutes he spent with the undertaker allowed the group of townspeople to gather around the horses. Malahide emerged from the building. Some ventured close to the body. One, more curious than the others, took a peak under the blanket.

"Hey, that looks like lawyer Bremmer, shot up something fierce."

Malahide stepped off the boardwalk. "Step away from there."

The man shrank back but still spoke. "That Bremmer?"

"Yeah, it's Bremmer. And he's dead. Now, make yourselves scarce. Come morning I'll be forming a posse to hunt down the one that killed him. So, get you ready 'cause we staying out till we get him. Now, scatter."

There was some discussion in the group as they dispersed to resume the activities Malahide's arrival had interrupted. Malahide took the Henry rifle and picked up his horse's reins. He led the animal up the street to his office. There he secured the horse and went inside.

Cletus held Rawls at gunpoint in the center of the room. Chrissie stood nearby.

Malahide eyed Rawls. "Where'd you find him?"

"Where Shawnee dropped him off. At the Tell." Cletus glanced at the rifle in Malahide's hand. "Where'd you find that?"

Malahide lifted the gun. "This? Same place I found Bremmer's body. Right next to it. Looks like your friend, Pearce, left a hell of a clear message, that he done Bremmer in." Malahide went to the desk and placed the rifle on its surface.

Chrissie looked at Cletus as a thought seemed to occur to her. "Do you think—?"

Cletus cut her off. "I reckon Shawnee did what he had to do."

Malahide faced them. "Well, Shawnee or Pearce—whatever you want to call him—you better hope he done left these parts, 'cause I'm taking a posse out in the morning to run him down, and we're staying out till we get 'er done."

Cletus smiled. "Somehow, I don't see that working out for you. Been tried before. He still be out there."

"We'll see about that." Malahide gestured toward Rawls. "You get anything out of this one yet?"

Cletus's smile became a grin as he looked at Rawls. "Oh, Rawls here, he a real song bird, all right. Ready to spill his guts to save his neck. Ain't that right?"

Rawls nodded nervously.

Malahide nodded. "Good. Let's hear it so's we can get this all sorted out."

———

A MONTH LATER, AT A campsite somewhere in West Texas, Shawnee hunkered down by a small fire. Evening was nigh. He went about roasting a rabbit skewered on a branch. The weather was getting warmer now as spring turned to early summer. Nights were no longer as chilly. Sleeping under the stars was not the chore that winter had made it. He looked forward to a pleasant rest this night.

There was a rumbling in his head, however, something that had not left him alone since he'd left the Tell and the Fort Worth vicinity. Loose ends bothered him, as strange as that seemed for a man who was constantly on the run. Many times, he'd had to leave situations suddenly, often without resolution. This was different. It involved people and situations he was close to, a part of. It involved Chrissie and Cletus.

His hasty exit after putting an end to Bremmer left questions unanswered, questions he was directly involved in, questions he sought unsuccessfully to resolve while he was there. They gnawed at him. He'd stopped in towns across Texas for newspapers that might speak of solutions, but that bore no fruit. There had been no mention of the Tell. He'd kept moving west after leaving the ranch, stuffing the persistent nagging of those questions.

This evening became the last straw. As he ate, he could not shut off his mind. He had to know. Yeah, it was dangerous. Yeah, he took a chance that his latest transgression might just get him caught by the law if he went back, but he had to know. Tearing off the last bite from the tiny bones, he chewed the meat and made his decision at the same time.

He'd go back because he had to know.

Getting up from the fire, Shawnee stretched and tossed away the remnants of the rabbit. He kicked dirt over the fire and stomped it out, then walked over to where Gray was tied. As he threw the saddle blanket over Gray's back, he spoke quietly to the horse. "We got to go back, Gray. My curious just won't quit." He lifted the saddle and set it over the blanket. Gray seemed to stand up straighter as Shawnee laced the cinch strap and pulled it tight.

For safety in backtracking, he camped by day and traveled by night. Functioning on meager food supplemented by hunted game, he made better time on the return trip than the idle pace he had set going west. Within three weeks, he reached the outskirts of Tell land.

He set up a makeshift camp at what he ciphered to be the property line and waited out the next day. After nightfall, he rode into the main compound and sought out the back door of the barn. He tethered Gray there and entered the dark barn quietly, settling into an unoccupied stall close to the one that quartered Cletus's horse. Scrunched into the corner closest to the stall opening, he tipped his hat forward over his eyes, folded his arms, and allowed himself to doze.

Rays of light signifying the break of dawn filtered through tiny openings in the wood slat barn walls. As the light reached his closed eyes, Shawnee stirred. He was immediately awake, a condition developed over his years of fleeing from the law. Rising silently, he stretched and waited for the cowhands to come for their horses.

The front door of the barn swung wide, letting in a shard of light. Shawnee squinted for a second as his eyes adjusted to it. A horse whinnied near the door. Several men entered to claim their horses, saddle them, and ready the start of their workday. Shawnee waited, hidden by the wide floor to ceiling post attached to the half wall of the stall.

Cletus entered the barn and walked sleepily to the stall where his horse stood. Releasing the retaining rope from across the opening, he stepped in and greeted the animal.

Shawnee took a step to the side, exposing his presence, speaking quietly. "How do, Cletus."

Cletus turned abruptly toward the sound. "Shawnee! What the hell you doing here? That policeman, he after you with a vengeance."

"Keep your voice down. I'd just as leave nobody but you knows I'm here."

Cletus took a step closer and lowered his tone. "Sure, sure, I savvy, but why'd you come back?"

"Had to get some answers. Then I be gone for good."

"What you need to know?"

"Well, I reckon I got my first answer seeing you walking around free. Leaving the Henry behind must a done the trick."

"Surely did, but they's no call you doing that."

"Had to be sure it fell to me, not you. Don't matter, just one more charge agin me. What's going on with Chrissie and the Tell? Can't find no news about nothing, no how."

"Working out just fine. After that Rawls fellow done told his story, Mister Grave had the Cattlemen's Association take the whole thing to court." Cletus leaned in and set his elbows to rest on the half wall. "Judge ruled that whole paper Bremmer drawed up about the ranch and Chrissie, that was... eh... null and void. He put the bank in charge of the Tell under his watch, and made Chrissie a ward of the court. Muley Purlow, he stepped up, and he's acting as her guardian till she of age. Then she take over running the ranch. It be hers then."

Shawnee smiled and nodded. "That's surely good news, all of it. I'm real happy for Chrissie. It's been tough on her."

"It has, but she her pappy's chile. She strong."

Shawnee nodded again. "Mighty well told."

"Something else 'bout Chrissie. That doctor-fellow been coming around, moonin' after her, visiting with her. Reckon he be sweet on her something fierce. And she ain't be chasing him away."

"She could do a heap worse, I reckon. Good for her."

Cletus leaned in. "Say, you should ought to hang around till she roll out. She be right glad to see you."

"Nope." Shawnee shook his head. "Bad idea. She don't need no reminder a me. I ain't looking to step on her chance with the sawbones. That's too important."

Cletus thought for a second. "Reckon you're right, but she surely will be upset she ain't seed you."

"Don't tell her I was here. She'll never know." Shawnee pushed his hat back on his head. "Well, I got what I come for. Reckon I'll be moseying. You take care."

Cletus straightened up. "Hang on a mite." He moved quickly to the saddle resting on the half wall across the stall and pulled the Winchester Yellow Boy from its holster. Stepping back to Shawnee, he held the gun out to him. "Here, take it. Make up for the one you... eh... done lost. Least I can do for you, you doing all you done for me."

Shawnee took the Winchester. "Thanks, Cletus." He looked at it. "Kind a looks a tad like the Henry, brass receiver and all."

"Surely do. So, where'll you go, my friend?"

"I don't rightly know, wherever Gray takes me, I reckon."

Cletus extended his hand. "Seeing as how I ain't likely to see you again...." He let the statement trail off.

Shawnee shook his hand vigorously. "Proud to call you friend, Cletus. *Adios.*"

Cletus nodded and smiled as Shawnee let his hand go. "*Vaya con Dios, amigo.*"

Shawnee stepped out of the stall and went to the back door. He slipped out and stepped up on Gray. As he dropped the Winchester into the empty saddle holster, he spoke quietly to the horse. "Time to go, Gray. Let's see what's out there."

He turned Gray west and set out to return to the outlaw trail.

DESPITE BEING A BORN-AND-bred New Yorker who lived most of his life in New Jersey, Bob Giel was a cowboy at heart and lived by the cowboy code. When most of the world today laughs at the quaint and seemingly antiquated concept of honor, he embodied it. Always faithful. Always loyal. Always giving his best effort. Always honest. And perhaps most importantly, keeping his word no matter what. Those values weren't just an act or an affectation, but something he worked at and recommitted to every day. Sadly, Bob passed away in early 2023, but his work and his ethos will continue to live on in his writing.

BOB GIEL

AUTHOR OF A CROW TO PLUCK

SHAWNEE

THE ADVENTURE BEGINS